The Lass He Left Behind

ROGUES OF MULL
BOOK ONE

JAYNE CASTEL

All characters and situations in this publication are fictitious, and any resemblance to living persons is purely coincidental.

The Lass He Left Behind, by Jayne Castel

Published by Winter Mist Press

ISBN: 978-1-991280-02-2 (paperback)

Edited by Tim Burton
Cover design by Winter Mist Press
Cover photography images courtesy of www.depositphotos.com and Midjourney

Chapter Three: Island of Mull poem (poet unknown):
https://www.poetrynook.com/poem/island-mull

Chapter Nine: Ailein Duinn traditional folk song:
https://en.wikipedia.org/wiki/Ailein_duinn

Visit Jayne's website: www.jaynecastel.com

He thought he'd forget her. He was wrong. When a battle-hardened warrior returns home from years of campaigning, he discovers that the lass he left behind never married—a lass who will be his undoing. Second chances and redemption on Medieval Isle of Mull.

After a decade campaigning against the English, Loch Maclean returns to the Isle of Mull to find his father dead and his lands in disarray. Cattle thieving is rife, and the isle's clans are at each other's throats. Loch's got his work cut out for him—but he's distracted by a woman from his past.

Mairi Macquarie is even more beguiling than he remembers, only these days, she's no longer innocent and biddable. These days, she's got no time for him at all. Or so it seems.

Mairi was heartbroken when the laird's roguish son went off to war and never came home. She got on with her life and tried to forget him. But now he's back, battle-hardened and cynical—and even more dangerous than ever.

The attraction between Loch and Mairi burns hotter than a Beltane fire, yet they both are looking for different things. He wants her to warm his bed, but what she wants is love.

And neither is prepared to compromise.

THE LASS HE LEFT BEHIND is Book One of an exciting new trilogy by Jayne Castel—full of flawed yet irresistible Highland warriors and determined Scottish lasses!

***

For Tim.

***

"The end of all our exploring
will be to arrive where we started."
—T. S. Eliot

1: GOING HOME

The Sound of Mull
Scotland

September, 1314

JAW CLENCHED AGAINST the biting wind and the icy spindrift that stung his face, Loch Maclean peered ahead at where the isle's dark silhouette loomed to the southwest.

Home.

His belly tightened. After a decade away, here he was, about to set foot on the Isle of Mull again. Nothing—not even the foul weather—could dull the thrill.

Aye, he'd given the best years of his life to following his king, to fighting the English. But the Bruce had been victorious at Bannockburn, and his army had disbanded.

Now it was time to go back to his roots.

He'd missed Mull's beauty over the years. Maybe its wild coastline, wind-blasted hills where sheep and cattle grazed, and sculpted granite peaks that speared the heavens would give him a brief reprieve from the restlessness that usually dogged him. Perhaps standing on the cliffs near his father's castle under the limitless arch of the sky once more, watching as a sea eagle soared overhead, would bring him the peace within he'd sought for years now, yet never found.

Another icy gust slammed into Loch. Hunching down, he pulled his fur cloak tighter about him and glanced over his shoulder at his three companions: Jack, Finn, and Tor.

Jack shoved wet auburn hair out of his eyes then and grimaced at him. "Rough enough for ye?"

Loch flashed his cousin a hard smile. "Scared?"

Next to Jack, Finn snorted. "Aye, shitting his braies … as am I." His friend's lean face was set in taut, grim lines.

The youngest of their party, Tor, clutched the birlinn's railing. The lad looked as if he was about to heave his guts over the side of the boat into the choppy waters of the Sound of Mull.

"I thought ye all said this crossing was an easy one?" Tor rasped.

"It is, lad," Loch replied. "When the sea's calm."

"It was calm enough when we set off from Oban," Finn pointed out, raising his voice to be heard over the roar of the wind. And it had been—yet no sooner had they left the busy port behind when the wind had kicked up, transforming the gentle swells into intimidating peaks and troughs. Finn's face then twisted. "Maybe Mull doesn't want us back."

"Aye, the locals might not be happy to see *ye*," Jack quipped. "I hope ye weren't expecting a hero's welcome."

Finn scowled, while Loch pursed his lips. His cousin's jibe was a sharp one, yet not a lie. It was said that the folk of Mull had long memories. "Well, the isle has got us all back," Loch said with a shrug. "Whether or not it wants us."

Shouting drew his attention then. Around them, the birlinn's captain and sailors were working hard to keep the small single-masted galley on course. The men bellowed at each other as they struggled to trim the sail.

A rogue wave hit the side of the birlinn, sending a curtain of cold water over its occupants. Loch growled a curse, blinking freezing briny water out of his eyes and slicking his wet hair off his face.

"Satan's cods," Finn muttered behind him. "At this rate, we'll drown before reaching shore."

"Aye, or smash ourselves to pieces upon the rocks beneath the cliffs," Jack added between gritted teeth.

Tor gasped out a panicked oath.

Ignoring his companions, Loch stared ahead. Water was now running down between his shoulder blades, and he braced himself for another freezing cascade.

The birlinn crested another great swell—and there, ahead of him, he spied their destination.

His breathing caught, a wild joy swelling in his chest.

There it is.

Duart Castle rose high against the leaden sky, its curtain walls impenetrable. The fortress perched upon a rock, guarding the sea cliffs and the rocky coastline surrounding it.

Loch's skin prickled. The castle's setting was even more spectacular than he remembered. Folds of grassy hills unfurled to the west, and rugged mountains formed a backdrop to Duart Castle, hiding deep corries and narrow glens where Loch had hunted deer as a lad with his father.

Da. Loch stilled then.

He wondered how the laird was faring these days. Their reunion after so long apart would be interesting. Would they lock horns as they once had, or had the years mellowed them both?

"It's too rough to land the birlinn at Duart Bay," the captain shouted, his voice almost drowned out by the howling wind. "I'll have to take ye to Craignure instead."

Loch nodded, even as his mouth thinned. It wasn't a long journey from the small port village to the castle—just over an hour on foot, and half that on a fast horse—but he'd been looking forward to alighting on the beach beneath Duart Point, the promontory where the castle perched. It was a wide swathe of white sand, where he'd once ridden his horse at a gallop, racing with Jack at low tide.

Ma also loved that beach. Something twinged under his breastbone at the memory, yet he shoved the sensation aside and turned his attention back to the coastline.

Aye, he wanted to land here—but he wasn't foolish enough to argue with the birlinn captain. And so, he watched his father's great fortress slide by and looked north instead.

A short while later, they rounded the headland and the port of Craignure hove into sight.

On a bonnie day, it was a pretty spot with sparkling white-sand beaches and a line of squat thatch-roofed bothies nestled under the rocky green headland. But today, with the wind whipping the Sound into a fury, as the birlinn's crew expertly guided her toward the rickety wooden jetty, the village appeared a bleak, windswept place, with its dwellings huddled together as if cowering from the vicious wind.

It took a few tries, for the swells risked smashing the birlinn against the dock, but eventually, the captain and his able crew managed to moor the galley. And despite the foul weather, a crowd of enterprising locals came out to meet the new arrivals, peddling sheepskins, pies, and skins of ale.

"Get yer hot mutton pies!"

"Ale to slake yer thirst!"

Their calls, snatched away by the wind, blended with the cry of seabirds and the slap of the waves against the dock. On the nearby beach, fishermen crouched on the sand mending their nets. Their gazes turned to view the birlinn and its occupants, tracking Loch and his companions as they disembarked.

Their curiosity didn't surprise Loch. Little went unnoticed upon this isle. He recognized a few faces and nodded to those he remembered. However, he'd only walked a few yards when two older women approached and started to pepper him with questions.

"Have ye returned for good?" one of the women asked.

"How many English did ye kill?" her companion added, eyes bright with interest.

"Who cares about the English!" A man hawking sheepskins shouted behind them. "Someone's got to do something about those devil-spawn Mackinnons."

Loch's mouth thinned. *Indeed.*

Ignoring the women—for he wasn't the type to indulge gossips—he strode off down the jetty, his companions following. His wet clothing chafed as he walked, and the wind dug icy fingers into his flesh, souring his mood.

"Loch ... wait!" Tor puffed from behind him. "Are we getting horses?"

"No," Loch grunted. "Ye'll have trouble finding them in a place this size."

"Aye, ye lazy young buck," Jack added. "Yer feet will have to carry ye the rest of the way."

Allowing himself a smile at Jack's dry comment, Loch cast an eye along the dock. News of their arrival had spread, for a crowd was amassing. Men, women, and bairns gathered at the end of the jetty, gawking at them.

Reaching the throng and turning left, Loch marked the veiled, wary looks on some of the locals' faces. He then caught snatches of muttering.

Not everyone was pleased to see the returning heroes back, it seemed.

Ungrateful turds, he thought, bitterness twisting under his ribs. *If it weren't for the likes of us, this isle would be crawling with the English.*

Suppressing a scowl, he headed south along the road that would lead him to Duart. A crowd waited here too, and Loch braced himself for another lackluster welcome. However, an old man with a chapped face and bright blue eyes stepped forward. His face split into a wide smile as he cried out, "Virtue Mine Honor!"

The words of his clan's motto hit Loch right in the solar plexus. His bitterness dissolved, and he grinned at the man, acknowledging his welcome. Over the past years, he'd met several of his clansmen among the ranks of Robert the Bruce's army, but the Isle of Mull was where the Macleans belonged.

Lengthening his stride, he cast his gaze wide, taking in his surroundings. It surprised him just how little Craignure had changed over the years.

The village was barely more than one road that hugged the water's edge. On his right was the thatched lean-to used for salting, pickling, or smoking fish. Three women salting fish upon a long bench inside it had stopped in their work to peer out at the new arrivals. A few yards away, the wainwright and cooper's workshops sat side-by-side.

Farther on, the village's only alehouse, *The Craignure Inn,* sat at the southern edge of the village, and it was exactly as he remembered it—a solid two-storied whitewashed building with a thatch roof.

News of their arrival spread like wildfire now, running ahead of them. By the time Loch passed the inn, the fishermen, cattle drovers, and shepherds who'd been drinking indoors had spilled outside, jostling to get a glimpse of the laird's son, his cousin, and their friend: a trio who'd once earned themselves quite a reputation here.

Loch's mouth quirked at the attention they were attracting. Aye, he, Jack, and Finn had been troublemakers once, although his position as the clan-chief's son had made him largely untouchable. No doubt, some folk in Craignure had been relieved to see the three of them depart.

But that was the past. They'd all matured, and their wild days were but a memory. After years of bloodshed and violence, Loch was looking forward to putting war behind him, and to helping his people prosper.

His gaze lingered upon the weathered sign hanging outside the inn. He was tempted to stop by and get out of the cold for a while, to dry off by a roaring fire with a tankard of local ale. Yet it was getting late in the day, and they had an hour's journey before them. Best to keep walking. He wanted to meet his father clear-headed too, not with his wits muddled by ale.

His gaze alighted on the woman standing in the inn's doorway then—and Loch's breathing caught for the second time that afternoon.

His heart kicked hard as he focused squarely upon the innkeeper's daughter.

And she stared right back.

Heat quickened at the base of Loch's spine.

The years had been kind to Mairi Macquarie—she'd blossomed from a comely lass into a spectacular woman. Her face was a little thinner than he remembered, accentuating her proud cheekbones, while her tall, statuesque figure was fuller. The laced bodice of her kirtle showed off a magnificent bosom and hugged the ripe swell of her hips. Long peat-brown hair spilled over her shoulders and down her back.

He wondered idly if her hair still smelled of rosemary.

Loch's pulse quickened as old memories stirred.

He and Mairi naked together amongst the heather, lying upon his cloak as he wound his fingers through her thick hair.

Mairi on her hands and knees as he plowed her from behind under the wide summer sky, her lustrous dark mane tumbling down her arched back.

The heat spread to his stomach.

Life had moved on. They were all older—and hopefully wiser—these days, but some things hadn't altered, it seemed.

Mairi Macquarie still made his blood catch fire.

2: A BITTERSWEET MEMORY

HE HAD RETURNED.

All these years later, after Mairi had resigned herself to never seeing him again, Loch MacLean had just walked back into her life.

Of course, she should have expected this, especially following recent events—but she'd long ago pushed him out of her thoughts, and her heart.

Loch had become nothing but a bittersweet memory.

Until now.

Mairi stared at the warrior who stalked down the road, ahead of his three companions. Lord help her, he looked good, far better than he had the right to. Dressed in dark leather and fur, he carried a claidheamh-mòr—a great sword—strapped to his back, and a dirk at his hip.

She recognized two of the men with him. Loch's cousin Jack walked with the same swagger she remembered, his dark-auburn hair whipping around him, and Finn MacDonald still had that lean, hungry look. The last of Loch's companions was a lanky young man with disheveled pale hair—a newcomer to Mull, Mairi guessed, judging from the wide-eyed way he gazed around.

But her attention didn't linger on those accompanying Loch.

It was *him* who drew her complete focus.

The laird's son had always been tall, dark, and striking, yet age and life had given his good looks an edge. The years had put muscle and brawn on him, had broadened his shoulders. He still wore his dark hair long, although it was wilder than she remembered, spilling in damp waves over his shoulders, while a short beard covered his jaw. These days, he carried a masterful air about him, the supreme confidence of a man accustomed to leading others.

But it was his gaze that held her fast: a deep, dark 'night-brown'—liquid and intense.

He stared at her with a boldness that made her chest constrict.

Outwardly, Mairi kept calm, schooling her face into an inscrutable expression as she held his eye. But it wasn't easy to maintain, for her heart hammered out a tattoo and her palms turned damp.

Keep walking, she silently willed. Seeing Loch again had thrown her—she certainly wasn't ready to hear the rough timbre of his voice or respond to him.

No, she needed time to get over the shock of seeing her former lover again.

She needn't have worried though, for Loch Maclean didn't so much as check his stride.

He shifted his gaze from her, and the pressure in Mairi's chest eased.

Heat flushed over her then, and she curled her hands into fists at her sides. Aye, he'd just given her a look that could melt stone, but the man had stayed away for ten long years. He could have sent word to her in that time, yet he hadn't.

She wagered he hadn't spared her more than a few passing thoughts while he'd been away. She was nothing to him.

Mairi's jaw tightened. She should turn away, should go back inside, yet her legs wouldn't move.

Instead, she remained in the doorway, watching Loch continue on his way. And she kept her gaze upon his broad back until he disappeared.

"Mairi Macquarie hasn't forgotten ye, I see." Jack's teasing voice drew Loch from his thoughts.

He glanced Jack's way to see his cousin was smirking.

Loch cocked an eyebrow in response. "Why do ye say that?"

"She couldn't keep her eyes off ye, man."

"I'd say it went both ways," Finn commented with a sly, wolfish grin. "Didn't ye see the way *he* was staring at her? I'm surprised Mairi didn't burst into flames. Ye should have shoved yer way through the crowd and given the woman a homecoming kiss, Loch."

Loch favored him with an incredulous look. "And vex her husband?" As always, Jack and Finn's teasing washed off him. "She'll be wedded now ... with bairns too."

"I didn't see any clinging to her skirts," Jack pointed out, not ready to let the subject drop. "What if she never married ... and has been waiting for ye all these years?"

Loch snorted. "Ye talk rot, Jack."

His cousin laughed, as did Finn. Meanwhile, Tor watched the interaction between the three older men with a perplexed expression. "Was that woman yers once?" he asked.

Loch shrugged. "Aye ... for a spell."

"She's bonnie. I'm surprised ye didn't return for her."

Loch harrumphed. "I had better things to do, lad."

Aye, he had, like making a name for himself and serving king and country.

Taking the hint, Tor didn't ask anything else. The men walked in silence then, leaving Craignure behind them. The wild wind tugged at their clothing and stung their cheeks as they followed the familiar road between the port and Duart Castle that wound along the lonely Morven peninsula.

Loch walked ahead of his companions, deliberately giving himself time alone so he could marshal his thoughts.

He'd already decided to ask Iain Maclean for the role of Captain of the Duart Guard. It would give him independence while allowing him to play a vital role in the castle's defenses. After all, leading soldiers was what he excelled at.

Loch pursed his lips then. He was used to being the one in charge and wasn't looking forward to having to take orders from the old man once more.

Despite the relentless wind, the walk along the cliffs was invigorating. He drew the salty air deep into his lungs and soaked in the untamed beauty of his surroundings: the waves that foamed against the rocks below, the velvet-green hills, and the vast brooding sky.

He sought to regain his equilibrium, for—despite his careless words to the others—locking gazes with Mairi *had* knocked him off balance.

I'm surprised ye didn't return for her.

Loch's jaw flexed. Of course, Tor would think such a thing. The lad was soft-hearted.

A woman had to know her place. She warmed a man's bed, looked after his home, and raised his bairns—but she didn't dictate his future. Loch certainly wouldn't give up his freedom over her.

And yet, Mairi had been his one weakness. All those years ago, he'd risked losing himself in her.

But when the Bruce had sent out the call, rallying swords and spears to his cause, Loch had disentangled himself from the web she'd spun around him. He'd cut himself free and hadn't regretted it.

They spied the castle a long while before they approached its high curtain walls. The fortress was more vulnerable on its landward side, and so the walls facing west were nearly thirty feet high and ten feet thick.

Once more, the sight of Duart made the hair on the back of Loch's arms prickle. He'd visited many castles over the past years, including the mighty Stirling Castle, yet none called to him the way this one did. The stronghold's vantage point, overlooking the water between the isle and the mainland, gave it a unique presence.

The four men walked over bare hills, where hardy sheep grazed, and past tiny Duart village—a scattering of cottages—before making their way up the incline. Ahead, the gatehouse loomed over a great stone arch.

The guards on the walls saw them coming.

"Who goes there?" One of them shouted down, a suspicious gaze viewing the new arrivals beneath a gleaming domed helmet.

Loch stopped before the gates, his chin lifting so he could look the guard in the face. He was glad to see his father took the security of his castle seriously. Time was, he'd left the gates open all day, closing them only between dusk and dawn. However, even though he'd been away a while, news had reached Loch about the worsening of relations between the Macleans and their neighbors, the Mackinnons.

His brow furrowed. Even a long absence hadn't softened his attitude toward their clan rivals. Like many of the Macleans, he believed the Mackinnons were a blight on this isle—one his father had struggled with for years. He'd hoped the old man would have dealt with them, yet the whoresons were still causing trouble.

"It's Loch Maclean," he called back, enjoying the shock that rippled across the guard's face. "Open the gate."

"Aye," the man gasped. "Welcome home!" He then ducked away, and Loch shared a wry look with his cousin.

"Feels strange, doesn't it?" Jack murmured, his fern-green eyes veiling. "To come back here ... after everything we've seen and done."

Loch harrumphed. "Aye. It's as if the passing of time hasn't touched this place."

"Some things *will* have changed, rest assured," Finn replied ominously. "Ye both know it."

The gate rumbled open then, and Loch moved forward, striding through under the shadow of the gatehouse and into the outer courtyard beyond.

Fowl pecked at grain on the cobbles, while two lads loaded muck onto a wooden cart in front of the stables. In one corner of the courtyard, the door to the chapel was open, while the clang of iron from the nearby smith's forge echoed on stone. The rise and fall of voices greeted them.

Loch's mouth lifted at the corners, even as warmth suffused his chest. Finn was wrong; Duart looked exactly as it had when he'd left it.

His gaze traveled then to the keep, which rose above them.

No doubt, word had been sent to his father of his arrival. He wouldn't go looking for the laird. Instead, he'd wait out here to receive him. Best to start as he meant to go on—best to *show* he was his own man these days.

Loch continued to survey his surroundings as he waited.

He spied a black-robed figure emerge from the chapel then. Tall and spare, with an angular face and a sharp gaze, Father Hector didn't look any different either. Loch had never been the god-fearing sort, much to the chaplain's chagrin. They hadn't gotten on well in the past. As such, neither man smiled when their gazes met.

Indeed, Father Hector wore a grave expression this afternoon, his dark brows knitted together.

Loch's gaze narrowed. He didn't expect the chaplain to throw his arms around him, yet the man looked as if he'd just swallowed vinegar.

"Loch!"

A woman's voice hailed him then, and Loch glanced away from Father Hector.

He'd expected to see his father emerge from the archway leading into the keep—a big, burly man with greying blond hair—but instead, a lissome figure, clad in a dove-grey kirtle, hurried down the steps. The woman had pale hair pulled back in a long braid and a woolen shawl around her shoulders. And as she crossed the courtyard toward him, Loch noted her determined expression, jaunty walk—and that she carried a dirk at her hip.

Behind him, he heard Finn's muttered oath.

Loch cocked an eyebrow. "Astrid?"

"Aye, brother," she replied, nearing him. "Do ye not recognize me?"

Loch's lips parted as he readied himself to reply, yet she launched herself into his arms—the force of her embrace causing him to stagger back. God's teeth, for a wee thing, she was strong. His sister's hug was so fierce that his ribs creaked.

Astrid drew back, her cheeks wet with tears, her brown eyes dark with emotion.

"That's quite a welcome home, lass," Loch murmured, taken aback by her reaction. At five and twenty, his sister was five years his junior. She'd always worshipped him, although he'd once been irritated by the blonde sprite who'd shadowed him and his friends. In the years prior to his departure, he'd treated her dismissively.

He thought she might have harbored a grudge for that, yet she didn't seem to.

For his part, Loch *was* pleased to see her. However, he wasn't impressed that she carried a weapon. Astrid Maclean was a clan-chief's daughter; she had no need to walk around so armed.

"I'm glad ye have returned, brother," she said huskily, her gaze never leaving his face. She hadn't yet acknowledged either Jack or Finn. "I don't know how the news reached ye so quickly ... but I'm relieved it did."

Loch inclined his head, his gaze narrowing. "What news?"

Astrid's expression tightened, tears sparkling on her long lashes. "Ye don't know?"

"Know what?" His irritation quickened then. His sister was talking in riddles.

Astrid stared up at him, a nerve flickering in her cheek. Swallowing, she then cleared her throat. "Da is dead."

3: LEANNAN

DEAD? LOCH BLINKED, not sure he'd heard properly.

The auld bastard couldn't be dead. Iain Maclean was a mighty oak, one who'd live to a great age. This news knocked him off balance; it was as if someone had told him that the sun set in the east and not the west.

"He was never the same after Ma's passing," Astrid said softly, her gaze roaming his face, as if searching for something. "He hadn't been feeling well of late ... he was short of breath and tired all the time ... and then four days ago" —she broke off, more tears escaping and trickling down her cheeks— "he keeled over in the great hall." Sniffing, she reached up and rubbed at her face with her knuckles, valiantly trying to pull herself together. Astrid had always been tough, plucky—very much like her mother. It was disconcerting to see her so upset. "No one could revive him."

Silence fell in the outer courtyard.

A gust of wind hit then, barreling in through the open gate behind them, and sending dust and straw whirling.

Jack and Finn shifted, their boots scuffing on the cobbles as they no doubt drew their cloaks around them, yet Loch didn't move, didn't take his attention from his sister's face.

"I was so sure I'd see him again," he admitted after a lengthy pause. He was aware that his voice sounded wooden, yet the shock of Astrid's announcement hadn't sunk in.

His mind churned, trying to make sense of it. But after a few moments, his throat and chest tightened. Christ, this was real. In truth, he hadn't spared his father much thought over the years, yet he'd always taken it for granted that he'd one day hear the deep rumble of his voice again.

Astrid watched him, pain flickering over her face. "Ye were away for so long, Loch," she said, her voice barely above a whisper. "Da thought ye'd never return."

Loch stiffened. He didn't know why any of them would think that. Aye, he hadn't sent word all these years, but Mull was his home, after all. And Duart Castle was his birthright.

The full impact of his father's death hit him then, like a mailed fist to the gut.

He was now the Maclean clan-chief. This fortress and everything in it now belonged to him.

"I'm sorry, Astrid," Jack spoke up then, his voice rough. "That is sad news indeed."

Astrid swallowed, finally shifting her attention away from her brother's face to meet her cousin's eye. "Thank ye, Jack," she said huskily.

She tensed then, her gaze narrowing as it settled on someone else.

Loch stepped to one side, his attention following hers, to where Astrid focused on Finn. His friend had folded his arms across his chest, his mouth pursed as he stared right back at her.

It wasn't a friendly stare, and Astrid's look wasn't warm either.

The hostility between them wasn't surprising. There was bad blood there—and a decade apart couldn't erase it.

However, Loch couldn't focus on the tragedy that had turned Astrid and Finn into bitter enemies. He was still reeling from the knowledge that Iain Maclean was gone.

Jack nudged Finn, none too gently, with his elbow. "And Finn's sorry too," he growled. "Aren't ye?"

"Aye," Finn murmured, his lean face strained.

"Is something amiss, Mairi?"

Glancing up from where she was wiping down one of the trestle tables that packed the interior of the inn, Mairi's attention settled on where Alison stood watching her, hands on hips.

Her cousin's usually smooth brow was furrowed, and she watched her with a sharp look.

"No," Mairi replied lightly.

"Then why are ye cleaning that table for the fifth time?" Alison cocked an eyebrow. "Yer mind must be elsewhere."

Mairi straightened up smartly, realizing that Alison was right. She'd already wiped down the table in this corner. "I'm a little distracted," she admitted, moving toward where a stack of dirty plates and tankards waited on the tall bench that separated the common room from the kitchen and scullery.

"Aye ... seeing yer old leannan again will have come as a shock."

Mairi jolted as if Alison had stuck her with a pin.

Hearing Loch referred to as her leannan—her lover—made an ache rise under her breastbone. It brought back a host of memories and reminded her of the agony she'd suffered when he'd departed Mull. For weeks afterward, she'd been sick with grief. She'd always thought the term 'broken-hearted' was merely a poetic one, until she'd experienced it for herself.

But it was all in the past now.

"I should have expected he'd come back ... now that the laird is dead," she replied with a briskness she didn't feel. "Yet it was a shock, all the same."

"I saw the way ye and Loch looked at each other," Alison said then, a sly light in her golden-brown eyes. "Something smolders between ye still ... even after all this time."

Mairi snorted. There were few secrets between the cousins. After her parents had died, Alison had come to live with Mairi and her father here at *The Craignure Inn*. She was six years younger than Mairi—and had only been twelve when Loch had left the isle—yet she'd been one of the few who'd caught glimpses of the secret, and forbidden, romance that had blossomed between the laird's arrogant son and her cousin.

And she'd been the one to comfort Mairi after he left.

Suddenly, Mairi wished she could rub out Alison's memories. The lass wouldn't let things go. "We were just surprised to see each other," she replied firmly. "And that's all there was to it."

Alison pulled a face, making it clear she didn't swallow her reply.

Mairi left the common room then—before she could say anything else—fetching a pail of hot water from a simmering cauldron in the kitchen. However, when she returned, Alison was waiting for her, seated on a stool next to the bench. "Give that to me," her cousin said firmly, taking the pail of water from her. She then tied her long dark-blonde hair back from her face. "Sometimes I think ye forget that ye *own* this inn now. Why don't ye get yerself a cup of wine and tally yer takings?" Alison flashed her a smile then. "It was a good day."

Mairi sighed before nodding. She disappeared into the kitchen, returning with a cloth bag of the pennies she'd taken since opening the doors shortly before noon, and a small iron box, where the coins were stowed afterward. Pulling up a stool opposite Alison, she began to count, stacking the silver pennies in lots of ten.

The cousins worked in companionable silence, Mairi tallying the day's takings while Alison washed up, using a rough block of lye soap and hot water to clean the trenchers and tankards. It was Alison's nightly routine before bed once the tables had been cleaned and the wooden floor had been swept. Mairi would then lock up.

It was cozy indoors, with the crackling of the great hearth at one end of the common room and the creaking of the wind, pushing at the door and bolted shutters. They were sounds Mairi had grown up with—as familiar as the steady beat of her own heart.

Placing her final stack of pennies on the bench—it *had* been a good day, for, after Loch's return, locals had flooded into the inn to gossip—Mairi glanced across at Alison. "We've earned well, of late," she admitted. Indeed, autumn had brought an influx of wool merchants to Craignure. "So, I was thinking about doing some work to the inn."

Alison looked up, interest sparking in her eyes. "Aye?"

"For years, Da talked about putting a wing on the back of the building ... but he never got around to it."

"I think that's a fine idea," Alison replied with a smile. "We never have enough chambers to accommodate travelers during busy times."

Mairi nodded. "I shall start talking to the local builders and carpenters this week then." Her chest constricted. How she wished her father could be part of these plans. Until a couple of months earlier, there had been three of them seated at this bench. She and Alison would have been scrubbing dishes while her father counted the day's earnings.

Mairi swallowed as sadness thickened her throat, her eyes misting. Grief was a fickle thing. Some days she coped well, and it seemed she'd accepted the loss that had rocked her world. But then, sorrow would steal upon her like a thief and deliver a swift kick to the belly.

As it did now.

"I often miss Da at this time of day," she admitted, meeting Alison's eye once more.

Her cousin nodded, grief flickering across her elfin face. "As do I," she replied softly. "It's at the quiet times, isn't it?"

"Aye ... he used to sing to us as we washed up." Mairi's throat ached now. "Did ye have a favorite song?"

"*The Isle Mull*, to be sure. It was uncle's favorite too," Alison replied, her eyes now glittering with tears. Her mouth curved then. "Ye have a better voice than me ... why don't ye sing it now?"

Mairi sniffed, knuckling away an errant tear that trickled down her cheek. "I'm not sure I can ... I might start sobbing halfway through."

"Ye might ... but music helps with grief, does it not?"

Inhaling slowly, Mairi gathered her strength and began to sing.

"Isle of Mull, island of joy:
wave-washed,
sun-topped,
wind-warmed,
peak-blasted,
with glens tight with hazel and oak,
straths grass-tawny, stepping waterfalls,
and mighty Ben More of the eagles
set high over all."

Her voice was soft and low, much like her mother's had been. Mairi didn't recall a lot about the woman who'd birthed her, for she'd died when she was young. However, she remembered her lovely voice, and how she'd sung to Mairi at night when she couldn't sleep.

Mairi's throat and chest remained tight, yet something inside her loosened as she continued. She imagined her father sitting with them, his deep bass vibrating through the air as he sang. How he'd loved this isle, and how his face had shone with pride whenever she and Alison had asked him to sing this tune.

Isle of Mull, island of joy:
dream-held,
burn-foamed,
deer-scattered,
gled-soaring,
with such the exile wears his memories.
As life's wrack ebbs his brief mortality
he still sees the green-richness of Ben More
rooted in the seas."

Mairi's voice died away then, silence filling the space where the words of the song had shivered.

A soft smile curved her lips as she met Alison's gaze once more. Her cousin was right. Music had eased the ache in her heart. Athol Macquarie was no longer with them, yet while she'd been singing, she felt his presence. Now, she knew how to keep him close.

She was about to tell Alison so, to ask her if there was another song she wished to hear, when a heavy knock sounded on the door to the inn.

Mairi stiffened, her smile fading. "It's late for travelers to be arriving," she murmured.

"Aye." Alison's brow furrowed. "Maybe it was the wind."

The knock sounded again, thrice this time.

"That's not the wind." Mairi slipped off the stool and made her way toward the door, weaving through a forest of trestle tables.

"Be careful," Alison warned, lowering her voice.

"I will," Mairi assured her. Without her father's brawn, the two women were vulnerable here at night. Mairi still hadn't gotten used to dealing with some of the more awkward customers at the inn, especially the ones who got aggressive when they were in their cups.

Tonight, two drovers—both in ill-tempers since having some of their cattle stolen—had started shoving each other. What had begun as a drunken discussion about how those 'bastard Mackinnons' were to blame had taken a nasty turn. One of the men accused the other of spending too much time humping his wife when he should have been watching his cattle. Fortunately, the local smith and his husky son had been on hand to pull the belligerent drovers apart.

It had been a relief to see the last patron depart tonight, and Mairi was careful to bar the door tightly. Maybe one of them had forgotten something.

Halting before the door, she leaned in close before calling out, "Who goes there?"

A beat of silence followed before a deep male voice replied, "Loch Maclean."

4: BEYOND HIM

MAIRI FROZE. A moment later, her belly went into a steep dive. Loch Maclean was the last person she wanted to see at present.

Recovering her wits, she cleared her throat. "The inn's closed."

"Aye," he replied, a note of wry amusement in his voice now. "But will ye refuse entry to yer *laird?*"

Heat swept over Mairi then, her temper quickening.

Curse him, the bastard had only just set foot back on Mull, and already he was throwing his weight around. He was *already* using his new status to his advantage.

With angry, jerky movements, she unbarred the door and yanked it open.

Loch stood there on the doorstep, windswept, intimidating, and surrounded by darkness. Outside, the night had turned wild. The roar of the waves pounding against the nearby shore joined the howl of the wind. However, Loch had dressed for the weather. He wore a heavy fur mantle about his broad shoulders, and his dark hair had been pulled back at the nape. Up close, his face was both familiar and different. He'd been smooth-shaven years earlier, although the short beard suited him. Upon his brow, she marked a thin diagonal scar that slashed from the hairline to slightly above his left eyebrow—a legacy of the war he'd survived most likely.

Mairi raked an incredulous gaze over him. "God's teeth ... it's a foul night to be out," she muttered. "What are ye doing here?"

Loch's sensual mouth quirked into a half-smile. "That's a warm welcome, lass."

Mairi folded her arms across her chest. "As I said ... we're closed."

He inclined his head. "Not to me, ye aren't. I've stabled my horse behind yer inn ... and if ye have a chamber free, I shall be taking it."

"But ye just arrived back on Mull," she pointed out with a frown. "Don't ye want to spend yer first night at Duart?"

"Not particularly." His smile tightened a little, his gaze shadowing. "It's been quite a day, Mairi. Can I come in?"

Mairi's heart started to thump against her ribs. There was an intimacy in the way her name rolled off his tongue. He addressed her as if he'd been away for days, not years.

Cursing herself for not having the nerve to slam the door in his face, she stepped back and gestured for him to enter.

Loch stepped inside, ducking his head under the lintel, before rising to his full height in front of her.

Mairi's stomach swooped once more.

His dominant, masculine presence filled the common room, emptying it of air. Fortunately, though, Loch wasn't looking at her. His dark gaze swept the interior of the common room instead.

"It seems smaller than I remember," he murmured.

"No doubt, it does," Mairi replied, unable to prevent bitterness from rising in her voice. "After all yer travels."

If Loch marked her jibe, he gave no sign. His gaze rested on where Mairi's cousin had gotten up from her stool. "Alison Macquarie," he greeted her, his deep voice rumbling across the room. "Ye were still a bairn when I saw ye last."

"Alison had twelve winters when ye left," Mairi corrected him before kicking herself. Only someone stuck in the past would have a memory for such things.

"Good eve, Maclean," Alison replied before hurriedly giving him a curtsy.

Loch cut Mairi an arch look. "At least one of ye remembers her manners."

Mairi stiffened, heat washing over her.

Alison's gaze flicked from Loch to Mairi before she cleared her throat. "I'll fetch ye a tankard of ale," she said brightly, moving toward one of the barrels lined up behind the bench.

Silently simmering, Mairi shoved the door closed and barred it. Then, without a word to the laird, she walked past him, returning to her position at the bench.

Loch followed her before perching upon a stool opposite. Refusing to meet his eye, Mairi scooped up the coins she'd just counted and dumped them in the iron safe box.

"I heard ye lost yer father recently."

Loch's words, spoken softly, made Mairi shut the box lid with a snap and glance up.

He was watching her, his expression veiled.

Their stare drew out for a moment before Mairi replied, "Aye ... two moons ago." Curse it, she wished her voice didn't catch every time she spoke of her father.

"I'm sorry to hear that. Athol was a good man."

"Aye, he was," she murmured huskily, even as she eyed Loch, looking for a sign that he was merely saying what was expected of him. But there was no guile in his gaze. She remembered then, how well he and her father had once gotten on. Loch, Jack, and Finn had spent many an evening at *The Craignure Inn*. Most folk had loved Athol though, for he'd had a warmth that drew others in.

"I didn't know my father had died."

Mairi tensed at this declaration. "Ye didn't?"

Loch shook his head.

An awkward silence fell between them while Mairi struggled to know how to respond. "It must have come as a shock," she replied, her tone softening.

"Aye." His gaze shadowed then. Loch's eyes were a deep 'night-brown' that could almost look black in some lights. "I know it sounds daft, but the old man always seemed invincible to me." He paused before giving a soft snort. "But, of course, no one is ... I, of all people, should know that."

"I'm sorry he's gone … all of us in Craignure are," she answered. "He was a fine laird."

Loch nodded yet didn't answer.

Their gazes met and held then, the moment drawing out.

Mairi's pulse started to race. Loch's stare had always undone her. Years ago, when he fixed his gaze upon her, Mairi's wits would have deserted her.

Not any longer, she told herself firmly. *Ye are no longer a starry-eyed lass, willing to be ruined by the laird's wayward son.*

Alison appeared at Mairi's shoulder with a pewter tankard of frothy ale and handed it to Loch. "So, is the fighting done with now?"

"Aye, lass."

"And the Bruce no longer needs ye?"

He shook his head. "The Battle of Bannockburn was back in June … and now the English have finally been trounced, our king no longer requires the hundreds of warriors who gathered at his side."

Curiosity gleamed in Alison's eyes. "Did he—"

"I'll finish up here, Ali," Mairi cut her off with a wave of her hand. "Can ye ready a chamber for the laird? The large one at the end of the hall will do."

Alison frowned. "But I—"

"It's been a long day … go upstairs, and I'll be up shortly."

Alison's jaw tensed, her tawny eyes narrowing. Mairi could see she didn't appreciate being dismissed and wished to argue with her. But something in her cousin's tone stopped her.

For her part, Mairi was fast running out of patience. She didn't intend for the three of them to sit around discussing times gone by like old friends. Once the last of these dishes were cleaned, she would end this reunion.

Alison favored Loch with a nod. She then cast a scowl in Mairi's direction, threw her dishcloth down on the bench, and stalked off.

Mairi and Loch sat there, listening to the creak of her feet on the stairs. It was only when they heard the slam of a door upstairs that Loch finally spoke. "So ... ye run the inn yerself these days?"

Mairi gave a stiff nod.

"It's not a usual role for a woman."

"My father loved this inn," she replied, her tone clipped. "And I'm determined to keep it running in his memory."

A furrow appeared between his dark brows. "Don't the local lads give ye trouble?"

"Sometimes ... but I can deal with them." Brave words indeed—and spoken with deliberate carelessness—yet not entirely true. Unfortunately, Mairi and Alison often had to deal with lecherous comments and wandering hands these days.

Mairi wouldn't admit such to this man though.

Loch lifted the tankard to his lips and took a deep draft. When he lowered it, his gaze speared hers once more. "I'll admit, I thought to find ye wedded with a brood of bairns by now." Mairi's grip tightened on the tankard she was now washing, yet Loch continued, "Why are ye still alone?"

Her pulse started thundering in her ears. How dare he ask her that? It was none of his business. She wanted to throw a tankard of dirty water over him for his presumption, yet to do so would reveal how deeply he'd wounded her all those years ago.

Instead, she dragged in a deep breath and lied. "By choice. Da needed my help ... and I decided I liked this life too much to give it up."

It was a plausible excuse, delivered with confidence—she was pleased with how cool and calm her voice sounded—and Loch's eyes widened a fraction. "Didn't ye want a family of yer own?"

Dizziness swept over Mairi. She'd thought he wouldn't remember those foolish, eager things she said to him once. "Maybe," she said, her gaze narrowing. "But that was years ago ... people change, Loch."

Another lie. She hadn't changed. She still wanted all the things she had years earlier. And it cut her to the quick that she did. However, she'd rather have her tongue yanked out than tell him so.

His mouth curved, and through his closely-cropped dark beard, she saw his cheek dimple. "Evidently."

"And what of ye?" she asked airily, dunking a tankard into the pail of rapidly cooling water with such force that suds sloshed over the side. "Is there a wife out there somewhere … waiting to be summoned to Duart Castle?"

Aye, she was getting the hang of this. Loch Maclean wouldn't crack her like a walnut, wouldn't turn her into soft clay to mold in his hands. She was beyond him now.

"No … I've been too busy with campaigning to think about marriage."

And now? The question teetered on the tip of her tongue, yet she swallowed it.

Loch was in his thirtieth year, and now that he'd stepped into his father's role, he would need to find himself a wife: a high-born and well-connected one no doubt.

Mairi didn't question him further on the subject. It didn't matter to her whom he wed. Not any longer.

Her pulse continued to thud in her ears, taunting her, calling her a liar. But she ignored her body's visceral reaction to his presence and concentrated on finishing the washing up.

How she wished she was done already.

"Lady Astrid will be pleased ye are home," she said briskly. It was time they stopped talking about marriage.

He snorted. "Aye … although I'm not fond of the way she strides around with a dirk at her hip, bellowing orders at my men like a marshal. Ye'd think it was *her* keep."

Mairi couldn't help but smirk at the disapproval in his voice.

Catching her expression, he frowned. "What?"

Mairi shrugged. In truth, she admired his sister. The clan-chief's health had been poor for the last year or two, and in that time, Lady Astrid had taken a more active role in the running of his castle and lands. Astrid even stopped off at the inn for a drink occasionally, always with her guards in tow, of course. In Mairi's opinion, the laird's daughter was a natural leader. She wouldn't enjoy stepping down to allow her brother to take control.

"Lady Astrid has a strong will," she said after a brief pause.

Loch's frown slid into a scowl. "My sister has been indulged ... but things will change now."

Mairi tensed, her amusement fading. *How typical of him*, she thought. *He always liked to be in control.*

She wanted to tell him to let Astrid be, but she bit her tongue. Their family business was their own. However, she couldn't resist a jibe. Dunking the last trencher into the pail, she shrugged. "Rather than bossing yer sister around, ye should look to dealing with the Mackinnons. They've been causing no end of trouble of late."

"So I've learned," he replied, irritation creeping into his voice now.

"Aye, two dozen cattle have gone missing over the past year near yer borders with them," she added. Working here, Mairi knew everything that went on upon this isle. *The Craignure Inn* was where all local news ended up. "And they've been trying to draw the Macleans into open war. There was a bloody skirmish near Sàilean a month ago ... and they have stolen lands belonging to the Macleans of Dounarwyse."

"I know all this, lass," he muttered.

Mairi gave a soft snort. "Aye, well ... I look forward to seeing what ye shall *do* about it then." She dried off the last of the dishes and heaved the pail of dirty water off the bench. "Now, if ye will excuse me, I need to get rid of this dishwater." Mairi nodded to his half-finished tankard of ale, indicating that he should hurry himself up. "When ye are ready, I shall show ye to yer chamber."

5: DO YE REMEMBER?

LOCH WATCHED MAIRI disappear into the kitchen, pail in hand.

Her abrupt dismissal irritated him, yet he could not help but admire her proud carriage and self-possession.

Mairi Macquarie wasn't as sweet and accommodating as he remembered. She'd developed a sharper tongue too and had an edge to her these days.

But despite his annoyance at being hurried up, Loch couldn't take his gaze off her.

He'd stood outside in the darkness and gusting wind for a while before knocking, listening to the sweet lilt of Mairi's voice as she sang *The Isle of Mull*. His breathing had grown shallow as the song drew out.

During his many campaigns over the years, whenever he'd gathered at the fireside with his fellow Macleans, there would be someone with a good enough singing voice willing to entertain them with that song.

It never failed to make his pulse race, to make him long for his birthplace.

However, he'd never heard it sung as beautifully. The song had pulled at him deep inside and caused a fierce protectiveness for his clan to rise. He was their clan-chief now, and it was his responsibility to see them prosper.

Chest tight, he'd raised his hand and knocked on the heavy oak door.

Alone in the common room now, Loch lifted the tankard to his lips and drained the rest of the ale in a few gulps. The ale at *The Craignure Inn* was as good as he remembered: sharp and fresh. He wished for another, although Mairi had made it clear their conversation was at an end.

Loch put the tankard down on the bench and surveyed the common room once more. The lumps of peat in the great hearth were still glowing brightly, although they'd be out by morning if someone didn't add some fuel to the fire.

Rising from the stool, he walked over to the hearth and added another brick amongst the red-hot embers, watching as it smoked and then caught alight.

Why are ye here?

Mairi's question wreathed up, taunting him.

And it was a good one. He'd only set foot back on Mull and learned of his father's passing. He should be sleeping now. Why had he ridden through the stormy night and knocked on the inn's door after hours?

Because Mairi always made things better.

The realization was unsettling, yet there was no escaping it. Loch's return to Mull hadn't gone as expected, and in the hours following his arrival, he'd been restless, agitated.

Alone, with only his thoughts for company, he'd stared moodily at the fire in his father's solar. His sister had retired for the eve, while Jack and Finn had joined the guards in the barracks for ale and dicing.

Loch usually welcomed solitude—but not this eve. Eventually, he'd thrown on a cloak, descended to the stables, and ordered one of the lads to saddle his father's horse.

And then, before he knew what he was doing, he was heading north, along the coastal track, back to Craignure.

Mairi wasn't pleased to see him, but being in her presence eased the pressure building inside him. It reminded Loch that, years earlier, Mairi had been his refuge. She, more than anyone else, had understood him.

Aye, the years had given her a harder shell—and now that she ran her father's inn, she had a more worldly air—yet he sensed that, underneath it, Mairi was still the winsome lass he'd once known.

He was still drawn to her; he still warmed to the gentle lilt of her voice.

"Ye didn't have to do that."

That same voice hailed him now, and Loch turned to see Mairi standing behind him. She carried a lantern in one hand.

His mouth curved. "No ... but since I've imposed on ye this eve, it was the least I could do."

She nodded, her golden-brown eyes—the same shade as her cousin's—still wary. "Have ye finished yer ale?"

"Aye."

"I'll show ye to yer chamber then."

Without waiting for him to reply, Mairi headed toward the wooden staircase that led up from the common room. Loch moved away from the hearth and followed her.

And as they climbed to the first floor, he couldn't help but admire the sway of her hips and the plump roundness of her backside, which her rust-colored kirtle showed off. Her dark hair was still long and wayward, falling in loose curls down her back.

Loch resisted the urge to reach out and catch a lock of hair with his fingers, to test if it was as soft and springy as he remembered.

Heat ignited in the pit of his belly then.

It surprised him how strongly Mairi still affected him. In the decade they'd spent apart, he'd pushed her from his thoughts; indeed, he'd swived other women without guilt or remorse. He'd told himself that the tether between them had been broken, yet she was the one he'd sought comfort from. And just a short while in her company this evening had him craving to be close to her again.

They reached the landing, floorboards creaking underfoot as Mairi led him down the hallway, past half a dozen doorways.

The lantern Mairi carried cast a soft lambent light over the stone walls.

A loud rumbling noise reached Loch as he passed one of the closed doors. "God's blood," he muttered. "Alison snores like a boar."

Mairi glanced over her shoulder, her eyes glinting. Her mouth twitched then in the hint of a smile. "That's not my cousin, but Fife MacDonald. The wool merchant often stays here." She halted then, before the last door, and turned to face him. "This is yer chamber ... Alison will have lit the fire and left a candle burning for ye."

Loch stopped before her, his gaze roaming her face. The lantern's golden light highlighted the faint hints of red in Mairi's hair, the tawny hue of her eyes, the smoothness of her skin, and the proud contours of her face. She smelled exactly as he remembered too: of rosemary, of sweet woman.

His gut tightened, need coiling inside him.

Aye, he wanted *her*. More than another ale. More than a soft bed.

Stepping closer still, he did what he'd ached to do earlier: he reached up and caught a lock of hair with his fingers. Aye, it was as soft as he recalled.

Meanwhile, Mairi had gone still, her large eyes drawing wide. A heartbeat later, her breast heaved, tightening the laced bodice of her kirtle. Her cleavage was deep and lush.

Loch's mouth curved, and he leaned in, breathing in her scent. "Do ye remember how good we were together, lass?" he murmured. He released her hair then, his knuckles sliding up the curve of her shoulder to her neck. Lord, her skin was soft.

His rod stiffened, need quickening within him. Aye, women had come and gone over the years, yet she'd been his first. They had a history that couldn't be denied, and he wagered she was as delightful to tumble now as she had been then.

Mairi made a soft noise in the back of her throat as if she was choking back a moan or a sigh.

Encouraged, Loch leaned in nearer still, letting his breath feather across her ear. She shivered in response, and his smile widened. "I still recall how I took ye that day ... in the hills, while the breeze whispered through the heather," he murmured. "There was never a bonnier sight than watching ye lose control, listening to ye scream my name."

Mairi's throat bobbed, her breathing ragged now.

Loch's groin started to ache as memories rushed in. Her scent and nearness brought everything back. He too had lost control that day—the only time he ever had let himself go fully during coupling. Two days later though, he answered the Bruce's call and left Mull without a backward glance.

They were standing so close; all he had to do was shift his head to the right and capture her soft mouth with his. Yet he hesitated, drawing the delicious moment out. He wanted her to give in to need as well, to lean toward him, to give him a clear sign that she lusted for him as he did her.

Mairi closed her eyes, fighting the dizzying need that had set every sense on fire.

The devil take him, Loch was as dangerous to her sanity as he had been in the past. And her will was just as weak.

His low, deep voice tugged at her soul. It was beguiling, wrapping itself around her.

He smelled good too—the crisp, clean scent of his skin mixed with the earthier tones of smoke and leather. And the feel of his breath, softly tickling her ear, cheek, and neck, made her want to angle her chin to give him better access so that he could graze his teeth down her throat.

How her traitorous body wanted him, *ached* for him.

She almost felt sick with longing.

And yet she fought it.

Remember how callously he treated ye, she told herself, pushing memories of that passionate day amongst the heather away. *How he was unmoved by yer tears.*

Her focus shifted then, not to the happy, loving, sensual memories, but the bitter ones.

Loch telling her he was leaving, his face a dispassionate mask.

Her sobbing and pleas for him to stay.

How he'd untangled himself from her arms, as if removing a clinging vine, and stepped away.

How he'd turned his back, leaving her weeping on her knees.

Mairi's eyes fluttered open as she found her balance, her strength. Her pulse was racing, sweat dampening her skin, yet she forced herself to meet his eye.

Loch's gaze was hooded, his lips slightly parted as his chest rose and fell sharply.

The sight of him so aroused nearly made her waver. It would be so easy to give in to this pull, like a strong current drawing her out to sea.

But Loch Maclean's allure was a kelpie's song. And like that perilous creature, he'd only drag her down into the watery depths, to her death.

Aye, this man lusted after her, but that was all he'd ever wanted. If she succumbed now, he'd merely toss her aside again afterward without a second thought.

She needed to remind herself of that.

"I too remember," she whispered. "It's etched upon my memory forever, Loch."

"As it is upon mine," he replied huskily, his fingers tracing a path across her jaw. "But shall we make new memories now, lass?"

Mairi gave a soft, bitter laugh. "How good with words ye are ... I'd forgotten how persuasive ye can be ... how ye will stop at nothing to get yer way."

Her words shattered the enchantment he'd spun about them.

Loch dropped his hand from where it had slid to her cheek.

Mairi held his gaze, letting indignance and outrage catch fire. "Aye, that's right. I know who ye are, Loch. Ye can't pull the wool over my eyes these days."

His lips lifted at the edges, even as his gaze gleamed. "And who *am* I then?"

Mairi inhaled slowly. What a gift he'd given her—an opportunity to vent her spleen, to lay out all the ways he'd done her wrong, to list all his flaws. However, she reined the impulse in. His gift was really a trap. He wanted to see her lose her temper. She wouldn't give him the satisfaction. He wasn't worthy of it.

Exhaling, Mairi took a step back, creating much-needed distance between them. A chill silence settled over the hallway. They were alone here; only the flickering lantern she held bore witness to their exchange. "Ye are the new clan-chief of the Macleans of Mull," she said coldly. "A man who gave a decade of his life to war ... who has just lost his father. Instead of attempting to bed the woman ye likely haven't given a second thought to all these years ... why don't ye retire and let yerself reflect on things a little." Heart pounding in her ears, she then cut him a withering glare. "Goodnight, Maclean."

And with that, she brushed past him and walked unsteadily down the hallway to her chamber.

6: THE RECKONING

ALONE IN THE hallway, Loch blinked.

He couldn't believe it. The vixen had drawn him in, dangled him on the hook as if he were a fat trout, and then deftly landed and gutted him.

Her self-control was admirable. She wanted him; he'd seen how her tawny gaze darkened and her breathing quickened at his nearness and his touch. Yet she'd pushed him away—and managed to insult him without losing her temper.

Loch frowned then, irritation spiking through his chest. He didn't enjoy being bested, especially by a woman.

Nonetheless, Mairi had closed her door, and no doubt barred it against him. She needn't have worried though. He was neither a bully nor a ravisher.

Scowling now, Loch let himself into the chamber Alison had prepared for him, shutting the door behind him.

As promised, a fire crackled in the hearth and a candle flickered on the bedside table. Alison had also turned down the bed, ready for him. Muttering a curse under his breath, Loch shrugged off his cloak and hung it up behind the door.

I know who ye are.

Her comment vexed him. He didn't like the feeling of being unmasked and judged. Underneath his annoyance though, embarrassment flickered to life. He'd come looking for solace this evening but had pushed things too far.

Kicking his boots into a corner, Loch yanked off his gambeson and lèine before unlacing his braies and pushing them down. His rod stood up like a banner on a battlefield, demanding attention. Mairi might have spurned him, yet that didn't stop him from wanting her still.

Loch's mouth thinned. She'd told him to retire and think on things a little—but *this* wasn't what she likely had in mind.

Doing his best to ignore his throbbing groin, Loch kicked his braies aside and crossed naked to where a jug of wine sat. He poured himself a large cup and slugged it back, welcoming the heat that burned down his throat.

Aye, he didn't like being thwarted—yet the truth was that he knew their history as well as she did—and he knew why she was angry with him, even after all this time.

His mouth twisted then, and he poured himself another cup of wine.

"I never pretended to be a good man," he growled, knowing that only the surrounding walls could hear him. "I never lied to ye about who I am."

And he hadn't.

He hadn't promised Mairi anything—but she'd gone ahead and foolishly imagined they'd have a future together.

If his leaving had left her bitter, it was her fault as much as his.

Draining his second cup, Loch then climbed into bed, blew out the candle beside him, and yanked up the blankets. He lay then, staring up at the heavy oak rafters, where the light from the crackling hearth caused shadows to flicker.

It was late, but he wasn't tired in the least. His mind was too awake to allow his body to rest.

He'd always remember this day—although not fondly.

He'd made a mistake in venturing from Duart Castle tonight. He should have stayed there and faced his discomfort. Instead, he'd ridden to see the lass he'd left behind. It wouldn't have taken much effort to send her just *one* missive over the years—and yet he hadn't bothered.

He should have known there would be a reckoning.

Loch kept his eyes closed, recalling the huskiness of her voice and how the lantern light had played across her proud face in the hallway: lovely Mairi with her golden eyes, rosemary-scented hair, and the body of a goddess.

Curse it, his rod was still rock-hard, demanding attention. He'd hoped for a hot, sweaty tumble with his former leannan, to chase away reality for a short while. But that was not to be.

Nonetheless, his bollocks were aching cruelly now.

With a deep sigh, Loch reached down and took himself in hand.

Mairi was carrying a basket of fresh bannock into the common room when Loch descended the stairs. Three other men who'd lodged here overnight were seated at tables near the hearth, and she was busy serving them.

Upon spying Loch, her first instinct was to ignore him, in the hope he'd choose not to break his fast here and instead go outdoors to ready his horse.

However, a good innkeeper didn't ignore their patrons, especially one who could shut down her business if he so wished. And so, she halted and forced herself to meet Loch's gaze.

He looked tired. His face was drawn, his eyes slightly hollowed, as if he hadn't slept well overnight. Like the eve before, he'd pulled his dark hair back, securing it at his nape with a thong. Fur cloak slung about his shoulders, he looked ready to travel.

"Will ye have some bannock before ye leave?" she asked, her voice cool, yet polite.

Loch's mouth twitched as if her offer amused him.

Mairi frowned. How vexing he could be. Suddenly, she just wanted him gone.

"No thanks," he replied, to her relief. "I'll be on my way."

"Very well, Maclean." Mairi continued across the room to where Fife MacDonald sat. She then set the basket of bannock, cut into wedges, before the wool merchant. Usually, Fife would favor her with a smile and tell her how much he looked forward to breaking his fast at her establishment. Yet the grizzled man wasn't focused on her this morning, but on Loch.

"Maclean?" Fife eyed the man standing a few feet away speculatively. "Aye, so the rumors are true ... the clan-chief's son has returned, after all."

Now the two other men seated nearby were staring, their eyes bright with interest.

Loch didn't reply, he merely stared back at the wool merchant, his gaze narrowing. After a beat, he then asked. "I don't think we've met?"

The wool merchant grinned. "Fife MacDonald at yer service." He paused then, his head inclining. "And I'm glad to see ye home, Maclean ... yer father never managed to end the feuding, but maybe ye can."

Loch snorted. "I'd have better luck stopping the tide."

Fife's expression sobered. "Well, ye'd better sort out yer neighbors ... while ye've been away, Kendric Mackinnon has been stirring up much trouble." His heavy features twisted then. "The whoreson seeks to rule all of Mull one day, ye ken?"

Loch inclined his head, his gaze narrowing. "That's quite a claim ... where did ye hear it?"

Fife gestured to the basket of bannock. "Ye look eager to be on yer way ... but if ye sit down and enjoy the best bannocks on the isle ... I'll tell ye all I've learned."

Loch hesitated a moment before removing his cloak, slinging it over the back of a chair, and taking a seat opposite the wool merchant.

Meanwhile, Mairi's stomach clenched at the realization he was lingering, after all.

Fife flashed her a smile. "Better bring us more butter ... and more of that fine heather honey, lass."

Mairi favored him with a brusque nod. Then, turning on her heel, she stalked back into the kitchen.

Alison was busy there, flipping another round of bannock on an iron griddle. The nutty aroma filled the smoky space. Her cousin glanced up as Mairi entered, took one look at her face, and grimaced. "The Maclean has shown his face, I take it?"

"Aye," Mairi muttered. "I thought I was rid of him ... but Fife MacDonald is worse than a gossiping fishwife."

Alison snorted a laugh, yet Mairi wasn't in the mood to share her mirth. Instead, she stomped through to the spence and helped herself to a fresh pot of heather honey. Returning to the kitchen, she picked up a clay bowl with freshly churned butter.

Alison was rolling out another round of bannock, ready to be cooked on the griddle. However, she paused at Mairi's return and met her eye. "Yer reunion last night didn't go well?"

Mairi's mouth thinned. She'd avoided the subject so far this morning, although she should have known Alison would bring it up eventually. "No."

Alison's brow furrowed. "Did he insult ye?"

Mairi stiffened, remembering how close he'd stood to her in the hallway. How his scent, his nearness, his breath, and the rumble of his voice had beguiled her—until she'd snapped out of her reverie. "I'd rather not talk about it," she muttered, moving toward the door. "Actually, I'd prefer not to speak of *the Maclean*, at all."

Her tone was sharper than she'd intended, and remorse needled her, especially when Alison didn't reply. Nonetheless, she felt bruised after the previous night and didn't want to dwell upon it. She'd slept poorly herself, tossing and turning until the wee hours, and felt out of sorts this morning.

Returning to the table where Loch and Fife sat, she wordlessly placed the butter and honey before them.

The two men were deep in discussion now, barely acknowledging her.

Mairi didn't mind though.

"And ye should know that the Mackinnon seeks to ally himself with the MacDonalds of Sleat," Fife said, his voice lower now, as if he was wary of being overheard.

"How do ye know that?" Loch asked, his voice sharp with suspicion.

"I hail from Skye," the wool merchant replied. "And have just returned from visiting my kin there." He leaned in closer to Loch then. "He's on Skye at the moment, organizing a betrothal between his daughter and Aonghas MacDonald's firstborn son."

Mairi turned and made her way back to the kitchen to fetch bannock for the other men waiting to break their fasts. Her brow furrowed as worry tightened inside her, forming a knot under her ribcage. The Mackinnons were forever stirring up trouble. She'd grown up under the shadow of conflict between the two clans. But this was the first she'd heard of an alliance between the Mackinnons of Mull and the MacDonalds of Sleat: two powerful clans who could cause much trouble for the Macleans.

And judging from the scowl that had creased Loch's face, he didn't welcome the news either.

7: NOTHING HAS CHANGED

"TRAITORS. THEY WILL try to take our lands, I know it."

Seated upon a high-backed chair by the hearth in the solar, his father's loyal wolfhound dozing by his feet, Loch frowned at where Jack now paced the room.

He wanted to deny his cousin's words, yet he couldn't.

"Maybe ... if they are fools," he said cautiously. Loch's conversation with Fife MacDonald that morning had been preying on his mind, and upon returning to Duart, he'd called Jack to his solar to discuss what he'd learned.

Speaking to Fife had been a reminder of his responsibilities as clan-chief. He'd known he'd step into this role one day—and he was ready for it—but there was no time to waste.

However, Jack's response was so volatile that Loch was now questioning the wisdom of confiding in him. The Mackinnons were a burr up his arse too, but he was reluctant to go into this like a bull at a gate. Unlike his cousin, he didn't let hate blind him.

"With the might of the MacDonalds of Sleat behind them, they might." Jack whipped around to face him. "Yer father was once a leader to be reckoned with ... but ye heard Astrid yestereve. After yer mother died, he lost the fire in his belly ... and his ill-health just made him withdraw further from the world. We need a clan-chief with the balls to take on the Mackinnons." Jack's gaze narrowed. "Are ye that man?"

Loch's frown deepened. He knew his cousin had good reason to despise their rivals, yet his mouth was about to get him into trouble. “Careful, Jack,” he growled. “We’ve been away from Mull a long while … let’s get the lie of the land before we rush into conflict.” In truth, after years of campaigning, he wasn’t in a hurry to take that route.

Stretching out his long legs, he crossed them at the ankles, accidentally nudging the dog. Luag opened an eye and regarded him warily. The wolfhound appeared both equally fascinated and intimidated by his new master, as if he wasn’t sure what to make of him.

Loch glanced up to see a muscle feather in Jack’s jaw. “That’s easy for ye to say,” he ground out. “Kendric Mackinnon didn’t slay yer father in cold blood.”

Loch swallowed a sigh. He sympathized with Jack, but that fateful meeting years earlier—which had ended with Mackinnon slitting Baird Maclean’s throat—was far behind them now. Jack had to let it go.

Pushing himself to his feet, Loch stepped forward and placed his hands upon his cousin’s shoulders. Squeezing firmly, he then met his eye squarely. “Ye forget I *know* what yer father’s murder did to ye … how it splintered yer world.” Indeed, the tragedy had changed Jack from a carefree, happy lad to a reckless and angry one. Loch’s mouth twisted then. “I thought our time away would mend things … but clearly, it hasn’t.”

Jack’s gaze burned into his. His eyes gleamed now as old grief bubbled up. “Some things can’t be mended,” he rasped.

“What of yer relationship with yer brother … isn’t it time ye built a bridge with him?”

Jack shook his head. “Rae isn’t worthy of ruling Dounarwyse. He should have taken revenge on Mackinnon, yet he didn’t.”

Loch grimaced. “Christ’s blood … everything is still so black and white with ye,” he muttered. “Don’t forget Rae was young when he took over from yer father … and likely thought his choice was a wise one.”

“Don’t defend him,” Jack snapped. “My brother’s a fazart.”

Loch growled an oath and stepped back, letting his hands fall from his cousin’s shoulders. There were times he felt like smacking Jack's hard head against the wall—and this was one.

The door to the solar swung open then, bringing in a tall leather-clad figure. Finn's sharp-featured face was flushed, his hair plastered to his scalp with sweat. He looked as if he'd just come in from training—which he had, for today was his first in the new role Loch had given him.

As of yestereve, Jack was now marshal—responsible for Duart's stables and horses, and for discipline within the castle—while Finn captained the Duart Guard.

Astrid wasn't happy with her brother's decision, for aside from her dislike of Finn, she didn't want him to replace the men who'd served her father loyally for years, but Loch had ignored her complaints.

He ruled here now and could hire whom he wished. Loch didn't have any brothers, yet he trusted both Jack and Finn with his life. He'd wanted to show his regard for them both by giving them important roles at Duart.

Halting, Finn's gaze flicked between Loch and Jack. "Interrupting something, am I?"

"No," Loch grunted, taking his seat by the fire once more. "We're discussing what to do about the Mackinnons."

Jack muttered an oath, yet Loch pretended not to notice. Instead, his attention remained fixed upon Finn. "I learned this morning that Kendric Mackinnon is making a marriage alliance with the MacDonalds of Sleat ... with a view to uniting against us." He paused then, his head inclining. "Any advice?"

Finn's expression turned thoughtful. Unlike Jack, their friend could be relied upon to give rational, dispassionate advice. He wasn't a Maclean, but a MacDonald of Dunnyveg, who hailed from Islay rather than Skye. Loch liked Finn's cunning intelligence, and over the years, he'd never gone into a battle strategy meeting without him at his side.

"Call upon yer chieftains. Find out how they have all fared over the past years," Finn replied after a pause, "and assure yerself of their loyalty."

Jack spat out another curse. "That's a weak move," he snarled. "Are neither of ye man enough to take on the Mackinnons?"

Finn snorted, not remotely offended. Like Loch, he knew Jack's history well. At the tender age of twelve, Finn's father had sent him to foster at Duart. It hadn't taken long for the three of them to form a bond—or to get up to mischief together. Finn wasn't one to make friends easily, yet once he grew to trust Loch and Jack, his loyalty never wavered. He'd been living here when Jack's father had been murdered, and like Loch, he'd seen the change in Jack afterward.

Loch rose to his feet and crossed to the window. Outside, the sky was grey and windy, threatening rain.

Reaching up, he massaged the back of his neck. After a poor night's sleep, he'd awoken with a slight headache that was steadily worsening. His 'reunion' with Mairi had left him tense and out of sorts.

"It's good advice, Finn," he admitted finally. And it was: clear-headed and sage. Loch turned from the window then. However, he didn't look at Finn but at Jack, fixing his cousin with a hard look—the kind he usually spared for his men if they dared challenge his authority. "Ride to Dounarwyse ... and call yer brother to me."

A nerve jumped in Jack's cheek.

"That's an order ... not a request," Loch added, making it clear there would be no argument.

Jack glared at him yet held his tongue. Aye, he'd do as bid—even if it was under sufferance. Despite the bad blood between the brothers, Jack knew as much as Loch that they needed Rae Maclean's support. Dounarwyse Castle was one of the four Maclean strongholds on Mull. The castle defended the border between Maclean and Mackinnon lands farther up the coast.

Satisfied that Jack wasn't going to give him any further problems, Loch glanced back at Finn. "Fetch the chieftains of Moy and Breachacha too ... it's time we all worked together for a common cause."

Finn moved toward the door once more. "Right then, I'd better get going. Moy is quite a distance, but if I leave now, I can break my journey overnight in Ardura."

"Good," Loch replied before nodding to Jack. "Off ye go too, cousin ... ye should be able to make Dounarwyse by nightfall."

Alone in the solar a short while later, Loch poured himself a cup of sloe wine. He then looked over at the desk, piled high with his father's papers, next to the window, his brow furrowing.

While Jack and Finn were away, calling his chieftains to Duart, Loch wouldn't sit idle. There was plenty to sort out as he waited for them to return.

At his feet, Luag had sat up and was now scratching. Loch cast the brindled wolfhound a jaundiced look. "Ye'd better not give me fleas," he warned the beast.

Luag stopped scratching and focused on Loch, his gaze beseeching.

Loch dismissed him with a snort. His father had always loved dogs, although Luag hadn't been with him ten years earlier. He'd had a pair of bitches then. In truth, Loch found a hound's blind devotion vaguely irritating, while his father had enjoyed the adoration.

It was one of the many differences between them.

Cup in hand, Loch crossed the solar to his father's desk, his gaze sweeping over the piles of documents and ledgers.

His mouth pursed, and he glanced back over at the hearth, from where Luag was watching him keenly. "He was an untidy bastard, wasn't he?"

Luag gave a soft whine in reply.

"Aye, and he had a needy hound," Loch muttered. With a sigh, he settled himself onto the oaken chair at the desk. Then, taking a gulp of wine, he set the cup down.

His gaze went to a folded piece of parchment, fixed with a wax seal.

It bore the imprint of a castle tower—the Maclean emblem.

Without thinking, he touched the signet ring he now wore upon the little finger of his right hand. Astrid had given it to him the day before, shortly after his arrival.

It was the laird's signet—his father's ring.

Peering at the folded page, he stilled. It bore his name, scrawled in his father's hand. Loch's eyebrows shot up. His father had left him a note. How was that possible? Had he known he was about to die?

"What have ye to say, old man?" he muttered under his breath. "Wish to berate me from the grave, do ye?"

His father had always had a criticism of some kind to level at his only son—but only silence answered Loch, and his gut tightened.

With a soft snort, he shoved both the uneasiness and the folded parchment to one side. He didn't have time to read a letter from a dead man. He then dragged the accounts ledger close instead and opened the leather-bound volume. "Right," he murmured as his gaze scanned the page of scrawl. "To work."

A knock sounded on the solar door at that moment, drawing his attention. "Come in," Loch barked, irritated at the interruption.

The door creaked open, and his sister swept in. Dressed in a fur-trimmed slate-grey surcoat, stout boots upon her feet, and her hair mussed by the wind, she looked as if she'd been outdoors for a brisk walk.

Loch's gaze went to the dirk she still wore at her hip, and his mouth thinned. His sister's habit of carrying a weapon was going to have to be dealt with.

"Good afternoon, brother," Astrid greeted him, ignoring his grumpy welcome. "I've just settled a dispute between two farmers in Duart village."

Loch scowled. "Excuse me?"

Astrid halted, her gaze meeting his with a boldness that reminded him of their mother. "Aye, a squabble over pigs. It's sorted now though."

"Settling such matters is *my* role, Astrid," he replied, a warning edge creeping into his voice. "Not yers."

Astrid's mouth pursed, in the same way his own did when he was displeased. "I was doing ye a favor," she replied. "Surely, ye don't want to be bothered by such things."

Loch harrumphed. He didn't, although he wasn't about to admit such to his sister.

Astrid's attention shifted from his face then, to the desk he sat at. "Ye have made a start on sorting through Da's papers, I see."

"Aye," he grunted. "Did ye touch any of them?"

Astrid shook her head, her expression turning somber. "I was gathering the courage to tackle the accounts," she admitted. "In truth, it saddens me every time I enter this chamber. Everything about it reminds me of him."

Loch nodded. He agreed. This room reeked of their father. The great stag head over the hearth was a trophy from one of the laird's hunting trips. The sheepskins that covered the wooden floor were from his prized sheep that grazed the hills around the castle. And the shield and battle-ax that hung on the pitted stone walls were Loch's great grandsire's. His father had been so proud of them and had told many a tale of his forebear's bravery to his bairns.

The solar smelled of him too: a woodsy, smoky scent that Loch associated with his childhood.

However, he wasn't interested in dwelling on such details at present. Instead, his gaze returned to his sister, and he frowned. "Why do ye carry a dirk?"

Astrid cocked an eyebrow. "For the same reason ye do."

Her response was pert, and it vexed him. "A woman has no need to bear arms," he muttered. "Leave it to yer men folk to protect ye."

"I know how to handle myself, Loch." Astrid put her hands on her hips and eyed him. "I'm no longer a lass of fifteen ... and my responsibilities sometimes put me in situations where I have to show my authority."

"Not any longer," he countered. "I'm here now, and *ye* are the Lady of Duart. Take to the ladies' solar, as Ma did, and busy yerself with sewing and weaving."

"I'm not spending all day locked up in that stifling chamber," she shot back, spots of color appearing on her cheekbones. “Sewing and weaving bore me to tears. My skills are best employed elsewhere.” Her gaze flicked to the pile of messy papers on the desk. “I can help ye sort through these. It’ll be easier with the two of us—”

Loch slammed the ledger shut, causing the fine layer of dust on the desk to billow up and tickle his nose. He was tired of mouthy women. “Ye are not to touch anything on this desk,” he growled.

Her chin lifted. “Why not? I’ve helped run this place over the past years ... Da relied heavily on me.”

“Ye are practically a spinster these days, Astrid,” he said, pushing himself up and looming over her. “I can’t believe our father didn’t see ye wedded by now. What was the old fool doing, giving ye so much authority?”

Astrid gasped as if he’d just struck her. Her hands balled at her sides, her slender frame vibrating with rage. “How. Dare. Ye?” she bit out.

“I dare,” he snarled back, “because I’m yer brother ... and the laird of this castle.”

Aye, he was—and he needed to put his sister in her place.

“A title ye never earned!” she shouted, her temper snapping. “Ye walked out of here without a backward glance ... and never once returned to visit, or even sent us word to let us know ye were safe and well. And then, years later, ye stride in here and tell me how I should behave.” Astrid broke off there, her chest rising and falling sharply as she fought to rein in her temper. “I should have been the firstborn and a male. It was *me* who stayed behind and helped run this place, *me* who buried our parents. Duart Castle was beneath ye back then, wasn’t it? Ye always were self-centered and vainglorious ... and I see nothing has changed!”

Loch exhaled sharply, shocked by his sister’s stinging rebuke.

By the saints, the lass needed a good hiding for her waspish tongue. Her words were vicious, even more so for they held a vein of truth. He *had* left her to deal with everything. His little sister, who’d once adored him, now harbored a deep resentment.

He drew in a deep breath, readying himself to tell her off. However, Astrid didn't give him the chance. Swiveling on her heel, she marched out of the solar, slamming the door so hard behind her that their great-grandfather's ax fell off the wall.

8: UNSETTLED

LOCH GATHERED THE reins and nudged the stallion forward with his heels. Falcon—who'd been his father's prized dark-bay courser and now belonged to the new laird of Duart—clattered over the cobbles, passing under the portcullis, and out into the bright, crisp morning.

Impatience tugged at Loch as they reached the bottom of the incline beneath the castle. He'd awoken that morning feeling unsettled. It wasn't a new sensation. Uneasiness—the nagging sense that something was wrong—had been with him since childhood.

Some days the feeling was more persistent than others—and today, he couldn't escape it. After breaking his fast, he'd decided to go out for a ride. The only thing that took the edge off his restlessness, for a short while at least, was being surrounded by nature. Maybe visiting his old haunts would blow away the cobwebs and make him feel better.

Now was also the best time to take the opportunity for a short break.

Jack and Finn were still away calling his chieftains to Duart, and Loch had made a start on the papers on his father's desk. Astrid had also been temporarily dealt with. After their argument, his sister was wary of him. At supper the eve before, she hadn't worn her dirk. It was his first victory, although Loch sensed she wasn't done undermining his authority.

More fights lay ahead no doubt, but for now, it was time to find balance.

Urging the stallion into a brisk canter, he took the path through Duart village, passing women hanging washing outside their bothies. The smith, who was filling a bucket from the well, waved to the laird, and Loch acknowledged him with a nod.

He caught a flash of grey out of the corner of his eye then and realized that Luag the wolfhound had followed him out of the keep. The big dog loped after him, eyes bright, determined not to be left behind.

Mouth quirking, Loch shifted his gaze forward once more. If Luag wanted to join him, he could. However, the hound would have to be swift to keep up with Falcon's long stride.

Moments later, he turned the stallion off the road, onto the heather-strewn hills beyond. Falcon kicked up his heels, churning up dirt behind him, and they were off.

Cold air stung Loch's face, tugging strands of hair free from the thong that secured it at his nape, yet he welcomed the sensation. It brought his senses alive and chased away his thoughts.

He didn't ride along the cliffs today; instead, he headed inland, over the hills that climbed up from the coast toward Dùn da Ghaoithe, the sculpted ridge that loomed over the eastern side of Mull.

Falcon lengthened his stride, and Loch leaned forward, giving the stallion his head. Like him, the horse was eager to run this morning. Glancing over his shoulder once more, he was surprised to see that Luag was keeping pace, racing a few yards behind them.

They climbed steadily, and when Loch finally drew Falcon up, at the foot of the mountain, his mount gave a snort as if he wanted to keep going.

"Easy, lad," Loch murmured, leaning forward and stroking the stallion's sweaty neck. "Let's not overdo things."

Meanwhile, Luag sat down a few yards away, panting.

Seated astride Falcon, Loch gazed around, waiting for the tension inside him to unravel—waiting for Mull to work its magic.

Long moments passed as the wind whistled past and two sparrowhawks dived toward a corrie to the west, and eventually, Loch frowned.

The peace he sought still eluded him—even the beauty of his surroundings here couldn't settle his restlessness. If anything, out here with only his horse and hound for company, it grew sharper, almost as if it were trying to warn him of something.

"I'll bring peace to this isle," he murmured, making a vow to the whispering wind. "I promise."

In speaking those words aloud, he hoped to feel better, yet he didn't.

Irritation spiked then. Curse it, he likely wouldn't find the inner calm he sought until he'd sorted out their problems with the Mackinnons.

Jaw clenched, Loch drew his horse around and started for home.

"Another ale over here, woman."

Placing a dish of braised mutton and oaten bread before the fisherman, Mairi deliberately ignored Ramsay MacDonald's drunken bellow. Instead, she walked back to the kitchen and fetched more dishes of food.

When she returned to the common room, Ramsay's face was florid with indignance. The farmer worked a large tract of run rigs outside Craignure and was a regular to the inn.

"My cup's dry!" He shouted across the busy inn. "What kind of establishment is this?"

"Calm yerself, man," Alison muttered, snatching a jug of frothy ale off the bench as Mairi walked past. "It's coming."

Mairi tensed at the sight of her cousin weaving her way across the floor to where Ramsay sat with a group of friends—all local men as rough as him.

Her pulse quickened as she marked the hungry looks they gave Alison.

They wouldn't have dared to look at either woman like that when her father ran this place. He'd have thrown Ramsay and his friends out on their arses.

Her stomach hardened then. With her father gone, some of the patrons took increasing liberties.

"That's better, lass," Ramsay leered. "Yer cousin thinks she's too good to serve us, does she?"

Alison flashed him a frown. "Why don't ye cease flapping yer tongue around, Ramsay ... and return to yer knucklebones?"

"I can't play when I'm thirsty."

"Aye, well ... that's been remedied, hasn't it?"

Ramsay's heavy brows drew together at Alison's pert reply, and Mairi's heart began to thud against her ribs. Ramsay had a mean temper when he drank and had started many a brawl in here over the years.

Positioning herself behind the bar, Mairi kept an eye on them—readying herself to step in if necessary.

Meanwhile, Ramsay continued to stare Alison down. After a few moments, his heavy-lidded eyes hooded and he licked his lips. "How about ye sit on my lap for a bit, lass?"

Alison snorted. "I think not."

He made a grab for her then, but she was quicker, darting out of reach. Ramsay nearly fell off his stool, much to the mirth of his friends. His cheeks went dark red then, the color of raw liver.

"Watch yerself with him," Mairi warned as Alison reached her side. Her cousin's eyes gleamed with triumph, and faint spots of pink bloomed across her cheeks. She thought she'd bested the farmer, but Mairi knew his type. "Ramsay is petty and has a long memory."

Alison snorted. "Good ... let's hope he remembers his manners next time."

The door to the inn flew open then, bringing with it a blast of cold, wet air—and four newcomers.

Mairi's heart leaped as her gaze alighted on the clan-chief.

Nearly a fortnight had passed since his return to Mull, and she'd been hoping Loch would stay away from the inn for a long while.

Yet fortune wasn't shining upon her this evening, for Loch had returned. And this time, he had Jack and Finn with him. The three of them strode in here with the same arrogance of old, as if everyone present should bow to them. A fourth companion brought up the rear, the lad with long blond hair. The young man closed the door behind them, his gaze curious as he scanned the interior of the inn.

Those already seated weren't looking at the lad though, but at the tall, dark man clad in leather and fur who strode across the floor as if he owned it—and, of course, he did. However, rather than awed or excited expressions, most of those present were giving him wary, veiled looks.

Loch Maclean made for the table by the hearth where Ramsay and his friends had been playing knucklebones.

The look on the laird's face made it clear those seats were his.

Ramsay stared back, a disgruntled expression hardening his features.

Mairi's breathing stilled. Dear Lord, she didn't want another brawl in here. There had already been two this week.

However, to Mairi's surprise, Ramsay didn't challenge the laird. Instead, he muttered a curse under his breath, lurched to his feet, and staggered across to another table at the far end of the common room, shoving two fishermen aside so he and his friends could seat themselves.

Mairi let out a slow, relieved breath.

Alison cut her a quick look. "Do ye want me to serve the Maclean?"

Mairi shook her head, even as her belly clenched. She wouldn't let Loch intimidate her. He was home now, and she had to get used to him frequenting the inn. "No, I'll do it," she replied crisply. With that, she put four tankards on a wooden tray, balancing it in one hand, while she scooped up a full jug of ale with the other.

Then, head held high, features schooled into a polite expression she reserved for difficult customers, Mairi made her way over to the hearth.

"Ye have taken the best seats in the house, I see," she greeted the men cooly.

The lad flashed her an apologetic smile, while his companions appeared less contrite. Loch turned his night-brown gaze upon Mairi, pinning her to the spot. "Of course," he murmured. "It's only right, after all."

Mairi set down the jug in the center of the table before placing the cups beside it. She then started to pour the ale.

"It's good to see ye, Mairi," Jack said, flashing her a grin.

"And ye, Jack," she lied. In truth, she'd always been wary around Loch's smirking cousin. She suspected he wasn't as devil-may-care as he let on, yet he often wore an expression as if he were enjoying a private joke at someone else's expense.

"We were all sorry to hear about yer Da," Finn added.

Mairi nodded. She appreciated his words, although, she trusted Finn MacDonald less than she did Jack—even before the incident that had turned the whole community against him. Not long before his departure from Mull, Finn had stolen a boat and taken a local lass out on the Sound to impress her. They'd gotten into trouble, and she'd drowned. Finn had been blamed.

The folk of Craignure had never forgotten the tragedy or forgiven the young man who'd been fostering at Duart Castle. If the clan-chief hadn't protected Finn from their wrath, the locals would have seen him hanged.

Mairi studied Finn for a moment, taking in his lean features and sharp hazel eyes. Unlike some of the other villagers—a few of whom were glaring at Finn over the rim of their tankards—Mairi didn't blame him for Margaret's death. But there was no denying he'd been a troublemaker back then, in many ways the worst of the three lads. Loch had once told her that Finn was the youngest of five sons—the difficult one his father wanted rid of. As a youth, he'd had a predatory way about him that made her hackles rise.

She knew the trio were loyal to each other, but in her opinion, Loch, Jack, and Finn had once brought out the worst in each other. She wondered if the passing of the years had altered their relationship.

Her attention shifted then to the blond lad. “We haven’t been introduced yet,” she said, forcing a smile. “I’m Mairi Macquarie, owner of this inn.”

The lad nodded, his lips parting to reply, yet Loch cut him off. “This is Tor Gordon.”

“Welcome to Mull, Tor.” Mairi deliberately ignored Loch, instead acting as if the lad had answered her. “And how did ye fall in with these three?”

Jack snorted into his ale, while Tor’s cheeks flushed. Mairi guessed he was around twenty winters in age, although there was a shyness to him that revealed he wasn’t confident around the lasses. “Loch has taken me on,” Tor replied, pride lacing his voice. “He, Jack, and Finn are training me.”

“And in between learning how to fight properly, he polishes our boots, cleans our armor, and sharpens our weapons,” Jack quipped, slapping Tor on the shoulder. “Just as we did with the older warriors when *we* were wet behind the ears.”

Mairi favored Jack with an arch look before glancing back at Tor. “Aye, well, ye seem like a nice enough lad ... make sure ye don’t let these three rogues corrupt ye.”

Jack snorted a laugh at this, and Finn’s mouth lifted at the edges. Meanwhile, Loch frowned. Pretending not to notice, Mairi met his eye once more. “Are ye here for supper, Maclean?”

“It depends on what ye are serving,” he replied, boldly holding her gaze.

9: ONLY A MATTER OF TIME

MAIRI STRAIGHTENED UP, putting her hands on her hips. "It's braised mutton tonight. Will that do?"

He nodded. "Aye, bring over four suppers ... when ye are ready."

Their gazes held for a moment longer, and heat flushed across Mairi's chest. His lordly manner galled her, yet as laird, it was his right. Anxiety tightened her belly then. This man had a lot of power over her. The land this inn stood on was his—and, if he chose to, Loch Maclean could make her life difficult.

Mairi had no doubt bruised his pride during his last visit to the inn. Would Loch take revenge on her for spurning him?

She'd just commissioned work to begin on building the new wing, but one word from the laird could make the men she'd hired down tools and walk away from the job.

Trying to ignore her apprehension, Mairi forced a nod and stepped back from the table. She then turned and wove her way back through the press of tables toward the kitchen. Alison was pouring ale for two fishermen who now perched on stools at the bench—the only remaining seats in the inn. As Mairi neared, she realized the pair were grumbling to her cousin about a succession of poor catches.

"But doesn't the weather *always* take a turn this time of year?" Alison asked.

"Aye, but it's not only that, lass," one of the men replied ominously as he glowered into his tankard. "The

Mackinnons have been fishing our waters again … taking the best for themselves."

Alison inclined her head, her gaze narrowing. "Have ye seen them?"

The man nodded. "Only two days ago … three draggers, just north of here."

Mairi frowned at this news. The clans of this isle fished their own waters. However, the east coast had always been disputed. Traditionally, the Mackinnons worked the northern edge, above Dounarwyse Castle, while the Macleans fished the rest of the eastern coastline. Besides sheep and cattle farming, fishing was the lifeblood of this isle. Many of the local fishermen sold their catches in Oban on the mainland. It was a trade that Craignure relied upon.

"Ye should tell the laird, Dugal." Mairi stopped before the bench, drawing their attention. "It's a serious matter."

The fisherman cast a glance over at the table by the hearth, his weatherbeaten face then creasing into a frown. "Once … when he was in his prime … Iain Maclean would have wanted to know," he growled. "But will his son?"

"I'd say so," Mairi replied, favoring him with an encouraging smile. "Go on … I don't think he'll bite."

Dugal pulled a face. "All I remember of Loch Maclean is that he was a troublemaker who thought himself better than the rest of us," he muttered.

"Aye, well, he *is* the laird's son," Alison reminded Dugal, her tone wry.

Growling an oath under his breath, the fisherman heaved himself off his stool and moved away, in the direction of Loch's table.

Mairi watched him go, misgiving curling up inside her. She'd grown up with constant conflict between the Macleans and the Mackinnons, yet the news that reached *The Craignure Inn* these days worried her.

She wondered if Iain Maclean's death would make the Mackinnons bold, for Loch was untested as clan-chief.

Her worries grew as she cast her gaze over the packed common room. Craignure was a tight-knit community, and they relied upon the protection of the Macleans. She marked then how many of her customers kept glancing toward Loch, and the blend of curiosity and apprehension on their faces. They wondered if they could trust him, if he would look after them the way his father once had.

She noted then how some of the men present were still watching Finn MacDonald with a jaundiced eye—although if Finn noticed, he didn't let on.

Mairi remembered him as tough, the sort not to care what others thought of him. He didn't seem any different now.

Meanwhile, Dugal had reached Loch's table and was talking to him. The laird's dark brows knitted together as he listened to the fisherman.

With a sigh, Mairi turned her focus back to her work. She couldn't stand idle with the inn so crowded.

Tonight was the busiest in a while—it seemed as though every local man had squeezed inside to gain refuge from the driving rain. The rank odors of wet wool, leather, and stale sweat hung in the air. Even the pungent odor of peat smoke and the aroma of cooked mutton couldn't obscure the less pleasant smells.

Mairi had been on her feet for hours now, for the inn had been crowded since noon; her back ached and her legs were heavy. However, she had a while to go before she could put her feet up.

"Is something ailing ye?" Alison asked as she dished up trenchers of mutton while Mairi cut thick slices of bread to accompany it. "Ye look as if ye are nursing a rotten tooth."

Mairi flashed her a pained look before shaking her head. "Come on," she huffed. "Let's get this over with."

The two women took the trenchers of food across to the laird and his companions.

Loch broke off his conversation with Dugal at seeing their approach. As the fisherman returned to his seat, Mairi noted that his face had relaxed. Whatever Loch had said to him had been well-received.

Alison reached the table first, and Jack and Finn greeted her with smiles. Like Loch, they remembered her from years earlier. They introduced Tor once more, yet when Alison smiled at the lad, his face turned bright red.

Mairi said nothing as she served up the supper. Nerves stretched tight and belly clenched, she avoided Loch's eye and retreated from the table as soon as she was able, leaving Alison to chat with Jack and Finn. Her cousin, as confident and outgoing as always, was updating them on the local gossip.

However, even when Mairi was ignoring him, Loch still got to her. She hated how aware she was of him, how the sound of his voice made her breathing grow shallow. And as she made her way toward the kitchen, she tried to ignore the weight of his stare between her shoulder blades.

"I thought Mairi Macquarie was still soft on ye," Jack noted when Alison departed with the promise to bring them another jug of ale shortly. "But it appears I was wrong."

Loch grunted, making it clear he wasn't interested in pursuing this topic.

"Aye," Finn added, amusement lacing his voice. "She's feistier than I remember too."

"She used to look at ye with calf-eyes," Jack continued, grinning. "Now, she—"

"Enough," Loch growled, cutting him off. "Let's talk about something else."

Silence fell at the table. Jack smirked, yet held his tongue, while Finn raised a questioning eyebrow. His response had surprised them, but Loch didn't care. Mairi was off-limits. Both Jack and Finn could be callous when they talked about women—and Loch often adopted the same insensitivity—but when it came to Mairi, he wouldn't stand for any disrespect.

He wished *he* could steer his thoughts away from her. Over the past days, despite how busy he'd been meeting with his chieftains, she kept intruding.

Mairi had put him in his place—and his pride was still recovering.

“It’s good to get away from Duart for the eve,” Finn said then before taking a gulp from his tankard. “I, for one, needed a night out.”

“Aye,” Jack agreed. “There’s only so much talk a man can take.”

Loch made a disgusted sound in the back of his throat. “Listen to ye lazy bastards. Three days of meetings and ye whine like bairns.”

Jack shot him an incredulous look. “Don’t tell me ye actually enjoyed all that negotiating, smoothing ruffled feathers, promise-making, and oath-swearing?”

Loch shrugged, digging his knife into the hunk of braised mutton on his trencher. It was tender and smelled of rosemary and garlic. In truth, he hadn’t. As hoped, all three of his chieftains had responded to his call. Unfortunately though, none of them saw eye to eye initially; it had been an exhausting few days getting them all on-side—however, in the end, he’d succeeded. He felt drained as a result though.

Rolling his neck and shoulders, Loch attempted to loosen the tight muscles there. Tension always seemed to hit him in the back of the neck, causing a nagging headache.

“At least they’ll all stand with me now,” he said after a pause. He met Jack’s eye then. “Even Rae.”

Their gazes held for a heartbeat, and Loch noted the way Jack’s mouth tightened, and how his gaze hardened. He and his brother had been civil to each other during the meetings—an improvement on the hostility between them years earlier—yet their relationship was ice-cold. To see them interact, one wouldn’t know Jack and Rae Maclean were kin.

“Good,” Jack said tersely, his mood souring. “When the Mackinnons push south, we need to be ready.”

“*When?*” Loch held his cousin’s gaze, deliberately challenging him. “Don’t ye mean, ‘if’?”

Jack scowled. “It’s only a matter of time,” he growled. “Ye’ll see.”

Letting his cousin have the last word—for now—Loch took a gulp of ale from his tankard. After days of talking about the Mackinnons, he was sick to the back teeth of them.

Tonight, he wished to think about something else besides the yoke of responsibility that now rested upon his shoulders. He was a man who enjoyed a challenge—but all the same, his new role was testing him.

There was no settling-in period. From the first day, he'd been thrown into the deep.

His sister also continued to defy him. Just the day before, he'd caught Astrid discussing the collection of taxes with the bailiff. He'd informed the man that in the future he was to see *him* about such things, yet his sister had merely glared at him mutinously.

He needed to find a way to deal with Astrid, and once he had breathing space, he would. However, his father had left the accounts in a mess, he'd yet to sort the cattle rustling problems—and he'd learned that the Mackinnons were fishing in Maclean waters.

God's teeth, where to start?

Considering the mountain of tasks still awaiting him, Loch shifted his attention from Tor to where Mairi was chatting to one of the patrons a few yards away. As he watched her, she laughed.

It was the first time he'd seen her show real mirth since his return, and the sight caused a kernel of warmth under his ribs. For an instant—as he caught a glimpse of the carefree lass she'd once been—Loch forgot his worsening headache and the problems he'd yet to solve.

He forgot everything but her.

10: I WOULD GO WITH YE

AFTER SUPPER, TOR Gordon surprised them all by producing a bone whistle and playing a few tunes.

The lad was talented and played everything from lively jigs to haunting, melancholy melodies that made the fine hair on the back of Mairi's arms prickle.

Washing tankards at the bench, she listened to the lilting music, her mouth curving as she hummed along to it. Her father would have appreciated Tor's playing. No doubt, he would have burst into song and entertained everyone.

Sadness rose in a wave then, causing her smile to fade.

How she missed his reassuring presence. Athol Macquarie had been her protector, her champion. She wished she could have had one more day with him; she wouldn't have taken one instant for granted.

She could have done with his help too with overseeing the building of the new wing. The builders were polite enough, although they often spoke to her as if she were daft. It was much harder dealing with suppliers and tradesmen on her own.

"Sing for us, Mairi!"

Her attention jerked toward the fireplace, to where Jack had just called out. Next to him, Loch sat silently, watching her. She'd caught him staring at her a few times during the evening but had pretended not to notice.

Mairi's cheeks warmed, and she shook her head.

"Go on!" Jack urged, grinning. "It's been too long since we heard yer lovely voice."

Silence fell then, and all gazes swiveled to Mairi. Even Ramsay and his companions, who'd been making a noise in their corner of the common room, quietened.

"Give us a song," Loch said then, his mouth tilting at the corners. "Go on."

Heat swept over Mairi, and she silently cursed him. She'd sung for others often as a lass—but hadn't done so in years. After Loch's departure, she'd stopped.

However, his gaze was fixed on her in a silent dare.

Shoulders squaring, she gave a slight nod. Very well, she'd give them a song.

"Which tune shall I play?" Tor asked.

Mairi let out a slow exhale before clearing her throat. "Do ye know *Ailein Duinn*?"

The lad nodded, flashing her an approving smile. 'Dark-haired Alan' was a tragically beautiful lament of a broken-hearted woman who'd wasted away with grief after the loss of her lover. The woman had lost her will to live and died a few months after his death.

A moment later, Tor began a slow, melancholy tune on his bone whistle, and a short while after that, Mairi started singing. Her eyes fluttered shut as she poured sadness into her voice.

"How sorrowful I am
When I rise early in the morning

I would go with ye
Ailein Duinn, I would go with ye

If the sand be yer pillow
If the seaweed be yer bed

I would go with ye
Ailein Duinn, I would go with ye

If the fish are yer candles bright
If the seals are yer watchmen

I would go with ye

Ailein Duinn, I would go with ye

I would drink, though all would abhor
Of your heart's blood after ye were drowned

I would go with ye
Ailein Duinn, I would go with ye."

Mairi's voice died away with the last words of the song, and she opened her eyes.

Alison, who stood nearby, still holding a jug of ale she'd been about to refill patrons' cups with, had tears running down her face. Meanwhile, many of the men—including Jack, surprisingly—seated around the common room had glistening eyes in the aftermath.

But Mairi's attention didn't linger on any of them. Instead, she sought out Loch. She wasn't sure why she glanced his way. It was foolish really, especially while the sorrow the lament had roused still made her chest ache. But she couldn't help it. She wanted to see his reaction.

Part of her had expected Loch's face to be shuttered—for he wasn't one to wear his emotions for all to see—but instead, his gaze was shadowed.

Mairi's breathing grew shallow. Had her song moved him?

Raucous male laughter carried across the common room as the evening wore on.

Ramsay MacDonald and his companions had started another rowdy game of knucklebones, and as they downed jug after jug of ale, their cheeks became more florid, their voices and laughter louder.

Mairi kept a wary eye on them, serving them platters of bread and cheese to soak up the ale. She hoped they'd tire of their drinking and knucklebones and move on, yet the farmers appeared to have settled in.

As the hours slid by, a few patrons departed, braving the squalls outdoors to return home to their bothies. Others lingered though: Ramsay and his friends, and Loch and his companions among them.

Mairi had cleared away the last of the trenchers and was beginning to wash them at the bench when a burst of harsh laughter erupted from the corner.

She glanced over at the noisy farmers.

Her heart jolted when she saw that Ramsay had managed to pull Alison onto his lap. Her cousin had been passing by, carrying a tray of empty tankards, but he lurched forward and caught her by the waist.

Alison snarled a curse and drove an elbow into his chest, struggling to get free. In response, Ramsay roughly squeezed a breast with one hand, while he tried to get under her skirts with the other.

A red veil slid over Mairi's vision, washing away her natural caution around those who caused trouble in here. Alison was usually the one with the fiery temper, while Mairi was the voice of reason. She was also gentle by nature, someone who avoided conflict whenever possible.

Yet Ramsay had crossed the line, and she had to do something.

Her father wasn't here to ensure men like Ramsay MacDonald didn't harass Alison—so someone else would have to remind him to keep his wandering hands to himself.

And if she wanted the continued respect of the patrons, it had to be her.

Reaching behind the bench, Mairi's fingers closed around her father's heavy wooden club. Athol had kept it handy, to break up brawls when necessary. He'd shown her how to use it, although Mairi had never needed to.

Until tonight.

11: TOO GOOD FOR THE LIKES OF YE

THE CLUB FELT strange and unwieldy in Mairi's hand, but she pushed her discomfort aside.

Jaw clenched, she headed across the floor.

Out of the corner of her eye, she saw that Loch had risen to his feet. "Mairi." His voice carried a low warning she didn't heed. He might be laird of these lands, but she was mistress of this inn, and she wouldn't tolerate bad behavior.

"Let her go, Ramsay," she called out, her voice carrying through the quiet room.

Everyone had ceased their drinking and conversation, their attention turning to where Alison still struggled, her gaze panicked now.

Ramsay was still trying to get a hand under her skirts, while his other roughly kneaded her breast as if it were a lump of dough.

He leered at Mairi. "Only if ye take her place." He licked his lips once more, still holding the squirming Alison with ease. "And then, afterward, ye can take me upstairs and suck my rod."

That was it. She couldn't allow such an insult to go unpunished.

If Mairi let him get away with this, she'd never be able to hold her head high again. Locals would whisper about her, and other foul-mouthed letches would try their luck.

She prepared to lunge forward and swing the club at Ramsay—however, someone else got there first.

Pulling Mairi back by the shoulder, Loch pushed in between them. Then, moving with the fast, brutal precision of a trained fighter, he swung his fist at Ramsay's jaw.

A meaty thud echoed through the common room, and, with a grunt of pain, the farmer reeled back, releasing Alison.

The lass twisted free, and scrambled away, as Loch came at Ramsay once more.

The farmer had lurched to his feet, but Loch punched him in the guts, shoving him backward.

Earlier, before drink, lust, and rage had addled Ramsay's wits, he'd reluctantly deferred to Loch, giving up his seat. But now, he lunged at the laird like a maddened boar.

A moment later, the two of them were slugging at each other, knuckles slapping against bare flesh.

Still holding her club in a death-grip, Mairi moved back from the fray, leaving space for Jack, Finn, and Tor to wade in.

And they did, taking on Ramsay's friends with howls of glee. Fists flew, boots stomped, and elbows and knees gouged. The common room was in an uproar. Tankards and trenchers clattered to the floor, while tables and chairs splintered as heavy bodies collided with them.

But Mairi's attention didn't remain on Loch's companions for long. Instead, she watched, transfixed, as he fought Ramsay.

Loch kicked his opponent in the shins, slamming his fist into his stomach for the second time. However, Ramsay wasn't easy to bring down. Bellowing, he charged forward and landed a heavy punch in Loch's eye.

Loch grunted a curse and drove Ramsay back—sending a table and chairs flying—and slammed him against the wall. He then grabbed his opponent by the throat, pushing his face close. "Apologize to Mairi Macquarie for yer insolence," he snarled.

Ramsay glared back at him, his bloodshot eyes bulging.

Loch squeezed tighter, his expression murderous now. "Do it, dog!"

Ramsay made a strangled noise before croaking. "Sorry ... I'm sorry, Mairi."

Loch held him there a moment longer, while Ramsay gasped for air, and then released him with a curse.

The farmer crumpled to the ground, wheezing and choking.

Loch looked over his shoulder then, meeting Mairi's eye. The pair of them stared at each other, and, suddenly, the rest of the room disappeared.

Eventually, someone cleared their throat.

Blinking, Mairi glanced away from Loch to see that Ramsay's friends all lay groaning on the floor.

Loch reached up and wiped away the blood that seeped from a split lip. Already, his left eye was swelling. "Good job, lads."

Jack flashed Loch a grin. "Slowing down, are ye, cousin?"

Loch grunted. "He got a few lucky shots in, that's all."

"Thank ye," Mairi said, wishing her voice didn't sound so breathless. She glanced over at her cousin then. Far from cowed, Alison stood, hands on hips, viewing the bested farmers with a look of scorn. Mairi then nodded to Loch's companions. "I appreciate *all* of ye coming to our aid."

"That shit-bag insulted ye," Loch said, drawing her attention once more. His voice was low yet held an edge of menace that sent a shiver down Mairi's spine. He was glowering at Ramsay now, his eyes black in the ruddy glow of the firelight. "And he will pay."

"What do ye want us to do with Ramsay and his friends?" Finn asked then.

"Bind their wrists and tow them back to Duart," Loch replied. "Put them in the stocks in the village square ... and leave them there until I feel merciful."

Mairi swallowed, and despite that she couldn't stand Ramsay MacDonald, she suddenly pitied him. The hard look in Loch's eyes warned that mercy would be a while coming.

“I wounded ye badly all those years ago, didn’t I?”

The direct question caught Mairi by surprise. Glancing up from where she’d been pouring a splash of vinegar into a clay bowl of steaming water, she pulled a face. ‘Wounded badly’ was an understatement. “Didn’t ye see my tears when ye left?” she asked, carrying the bowl over to where he sat on the edge of the table in the kitchen.

“Aye,” he murmured. “But I must admit that I didn’t pay them much notice at the time.”

Mairi winced at his bluntness. “Well, at least ye are honest about it,” she muttered.

Compressing her lips, she surveyed his face. Loch’s eye was completely swollen now, an angry bruise forming. To combat the swelling, she’d given him a cool, smooth river stone, one she used to crush nuts and grain, to gently press to his injured eye.

They were alone in the kitchen.

Following the brawl, the lingering patrons had departed, while Jack, Finn, and Tor had done Loch’s bidding and dragged Ramsay and his cronies outside. At present, Alison was busy tidying up the mess in the common room.

Standing this close to Loch was discomforting, but as she’d assumed the role of healer, Mairi was able to focus on other things—able to ignore the scent of smoke and leather that wrapped itself around her.

Her brow furrowed. “Ramsay did quite a job on yer mouth,” she observed. Indeed, his lower lip was swollen and weeping. The farmer’s heavy fist had split it nicely.

Loch grunted. “Aye, well … the man has hands the size of turnips.” His mouth curved into a half-smile, and then he winced. “Satan’s cods, it stings.”

“Brace yerself, soldier,” she murmured, flashing him a rueful smile of her own. “This will make it sting even more.”

She dipped a clean cloth into the bowl of hot water and vinegar, wet it, and lifted it to his cut lip, dabbing gently.

Loch hissed a curse between clenched teeth.

Mairi's lips quirked. "I did warn ye."

"I think ye are enjoying this."

"Not at all."

In truth, she was. There was something satisfying in having him at her mercy, bloodied and bruised after he'd come to her defense.

"I'm sorry, Mairi," he said gruffly. "I know my apology has come too late ... and words are easy ... but I mean them."

Their gazes met and held. It was difficult to judge whether he was sincere or not, for he still held a stone up over one eye, yet his expression was serious.

Mairi gave a wary nod. It *was* too late, but she appreciated his apology all the same. She dipped the cloth into the water again and continued cleaning his split lip. Tension vibrated from Loch as she did so, although he swallowed his curses this time. After she was done, she reached up and gently took the stone from him, lifting it from his eye.

Surveying the injury, she murmured an oath before declaring, "Ye shall have a shiner by tomorrow morn."

"Aye, but it was worth it." His expression hardened then. "If anyone else gives ye trouble, ye are to tell me. I'll deal with them."

Mairi nodded. "Ramsay MacDonald is the worst of the troublemakers ... now that ye have made an example of him, others will behave themselves."

"Good."

"I shall fetch some goatweed ointment," she said then, stepping back. "It'll help the bruising."

Going to the spence, Mairi climbed up onto a stool and looked through the small collection of clay jars she kept for healing. The spence was a good place to store such things, for it was cool, even on the hottest days of summer. Sniffing the various unguents, she found the right one and returned to the kitchen.

Loch hadn't moved from his perch on the table.

However, his expression was shuttered when she stepped close once more, dipped her finger in the ointment, and gently massaged it into the bruise forming around his eye. "I'll give ye this to take away," she said as silence drew out between them. "Put it on morn and eve ... but make sure not to get any *in* yer eye, or it'll sting like the devil."

He grunted at this, closing his good eye as she worked.

Continuing to dab ointment gently around his eye, Mairi became aware then of how close they were—for she'd unwittingly stepped in between his spread thighs to get a good look at his eye. The heat of his body enveloped her, and suddenly, it felt overly warm inside the kitchen.

Realizing that his nearness was drawing her in, like a moth to a flame, she swallowed. "I think that should do it," she murmured, cursing the sudden huskiness in her voice.

She went to step back then, yet his hand came up, catching her gently around the wrist.

Her breathing caught, and she froze.

Curse him, even his light touch sent her pulse wild.

Their gazes met, and Loch's swollen mouth curved. "Thank ye, Mairi ... ye always were kind-hearted."

Her belly clenched at these words. She was—not that it had ever done her any good.

In a valiant attempt to rein in her response, she shrugged. And then, gathering her courage, she replied, "Aye ... and too good for the likes of ye."

Loch nodded, even as his night-brown eyes shadowed. A heartbeat passed, and then he slowly let go of her, his fingertips trailing across the sensitive skin on the underside of her wrist as he did so. Mairi couldn't help it, she shivered. "That's right, lass," he murmured. "Ye always were."

12: THE ALLIANCE

STARING DOWN AT the page of the accounts ledger, Loch muttered an oath. Trying to reconcile the rows of squiggles Iain Maclean had scratched out was giving him another headache that only added to the dull throb of his black eye.

He then massaged a stiff muscle in his right shoulder; he was sore after his fight the day before.

In truth, he'd wanted to kill Ramsay.

He'd insulted Mairi. Over the past decade, Loch had killed men for less—nameless and faceless soldiers who'd had the misfortune to be English.

Only the fact that Mairi and Alison were present had prevented him from crushing the farmer's windpipe.

Loch leaned back in his chair, his gaze going to the open window. It wasn't the sort of weather to have the shutters open—for the sky was the color of slate and a chill wind barreled in from the north—however, he preferred to work on the accounts in daylight, rather than squinting by candlelight.

Indoors, the great hearth crackled cozily. Luag had stretched his long body out in front of it and was snoring softly, while, outside, the shouts and grunts of warriors training in the outer courtyard drifted into the solar, accompanied by the bleating of sheep on the hills beyond the castle.

They were familiar, and oddly comforting, sights and sounds, yet Loch couldn't relax—not with the Mackinnon situation unresolved. Aye, he'd assured himself of his chieftains' loyalty, but he needed more allies. Perhaps he could call on the Macquaries as well; they'd always sided with his father against the Mackinnons in the past.

Loch frowned. Whatever direction he took now had to be thought through. Gathering allies was one thing, but the moment he made an aggressive move toward the Mackinnons, tension would escalate. And then, before they knew it, they'd be facing each other in battle.

Until a few months earlier, violence had been a way of life for Loch. He wasn't afraid to get blood on his hands, yet he was also tired of it. He didn't want to lose clansmen to war or get caught up in a spiral that might put the people of his lands in danger.

Thoughts of Mairi intruded then, as they often had today, and Loch's frown deepened. The lass fascinated him as much as she ever had, and he wasn't sure that was a good thing.

The night before, as he'd listened to her sing, his breathing had stopped for a short while. The power in her voice, the raw emotion, had caught him in a stranglehold.

And a strange longing had unfurled like a fern inside his chest as the lament drew out.

Muttering another curse, Loch looked back down at the accounts ledger. *Focus, man!*

He was only halfway through reconciling it; the job was taking much longer than he'd expected. His gaze shifted then to the folded and sealed parchment that still sat on the top of his father's papers. Picking it up, Loch turned the missive over in his hands before running his fingertip over the wax seal. He hadn't opened it yet, and he wasn't sure he would.

His mouth thinned. Over the past fortnight, he'd often glanced at the letter and wondered what the laird had written. Would the missive be full of recriminations for all the ways his son had failed him, or would it be full of the self-pity of a dying man? Either way, he didn't need to read it.

"Brother ... we have visitors."

Loch glanced up from his brooding to find Astrid standing in the open doorway to the solar. Arms folded across her chest, she viewed him coolly.

Loch frowned at her. "Who?"

"Kendric Mackinnon."

Loch's spine snapped straight. "What?" he growled. "The clan-chief?"

"Aye. He's waiting outside the gate ... says he comes in peace" —her mouth twisted at this— "and wishes to meet with the new laird of Duart."

Loch shoved back his chair and rose to his feet.

Astrid inclined her head, her dark eyes, the same hue as his own, narrowing. "Ye aren't going to meet him, are ye?" There was a challenge in her voice. He could feel her disapproval suffusing the chamber.

"Aye." Loch strode across the solar toward his sister. "And so are *ye*."

Seated in the great hall of Duart Castle, upon the clan-chief's oaken chair with a tower carved into its high back, Loch surveyed his guests with a deliberately veiled gaze.

His rival, Kendric Mackinnon, sat a few feet away, flanked by his son and daughter. Four of their escort—warriors in chain mail shirts, sashes of blocky green and red plaid across their chests—stood behind them. The Mackinnon had brought a party of twenty warriors south, but Loch insisted the rest of their group wait outside while they met.

The Maclean welcome reception was a sparse one.

Their family was small indeed these days, something that weakened it. Astrid sat to Loch's left, while Jack and Finn stood on either side of him, flanking his chair.

Loch had been wary of allowing Jack to attend the meeting. His cousin was a hothead at the best of times. This situation would test him, for his father's murderer sat a few feet away from where he stood, within striking distance. Vengeance could be his. However, Loch had warned Jack to keep his temper leashed.

The Mackinnons had made themselves vulnerable in coming here, and he wouldn't break with Highland tradition by betraying their trust.

Silence echoed through the wide hall as both parties regarded each other.

Outside, the wind rattled the shutters, and the flames in the hearth guttered with each gust. The great hall of Duart was a cavernous rectangular space with a high wood-beamed ceiling and exposed stone walls. Fresh reeds covered the floor. Meanwhile, Luag sat faithfully at Loch's feet. The hound's devotion was both gratifying and irritating; wherever he went within the keep these days, it followed, and of late, Luag watched him with adoring eyes.

Loch had no idea why he'd earned such devotion.

"Ye've been in the wars, Maclean," The Mackinnon eventually observed, his mouth lifting into a cool smile as his gaze took in the state of Loch's face.

Loch nodded. "Aye," he murmured, deliberately not elaborating on how he'd gotten the split lip and black eye. "Plenty of them."

Mackinnon gave a soft snort. "Apologies for not sending word ahead of our arrival."

In contrast to his words, the clan-chief didn't sound remotely contrite.

Anger hardened Loch's gut. The bastard had a nerve. Iain Maclean would turn in his grave to learn that his nemesis had ridden here so boldly and was now sitting in this hall, drinking his wine. The Mackinnons had been sly too, taking the backroads and avoiding Maclean villages, where someone would have seen them and sent word ahead.

Loch steepled his fingers in front of him. "If I'd known ye were on yer way, we could have given ye a proper Maclean welcome," he said, his voice flat.

"There was no time," Kendric Mackinnon replied smoothly, his silvery gaze never leaving Loch's face. "Once I heard that Iain was dead, I felt compelled to make this trip. We had our differences, but I thought he'd live for a while yet. I wish to give my condolences" —he paused then, his sharp-featured face schooling itself into a diplomat's expression— "and to see if our two clans might bury the hatchet."

Loch leaned back in his chair, crossing one booted ankle across the knee. Now, the man had his interest.

Mackinnon leaned forward, his stare growing bright as he waited for Loch's answer.

It wasn't forthcoming. The balance of power had shifted in the hall, and Loch would enjoy it. He was new to this role, yet his meetings over the past days had taught him the value of not allowing others to set the pace.

Biding his time, he lifted his goblet and took a sip. The wine stung his lip, yet he welcomed the pain. It kept his senses sharp. "Ye have been quite the peace-weaver of late, haven't ye?" he said finally.

Mackinnon's silvery gaze narrowed.

"Word has reached me that ye recently returned from a visit to the Isle of Skye," Loch continued. "Aonghas MacDonald of Sleat is now an ally, is he not? Now that ye have betrothed yer daughter to his son." His gaze flicked to Mackinnon's daughter, Tara. She was a striking, if haughty-looking, lass with creamy skin, silver-grey eyes, and flame-red hair. Unlike her father, whose fiery-red mane was dulled by strands of grey, both his son and daughter had hair of the brightest hue Loch had ever seen.

The clan-chief's gaze hardened. "What of it?"

Loch fixed him with a level look. "Why does a man who comes to me speaking of peace ensure he allies himself first with the MacDonalds?"

To his credit, Kendric Mackinnon didn't look remotely bothered by the directness of his question. This was the first time they'd ever met, but the man wore self-confidence like a comfortable cloak. The moment they'd introduced themselves in the outer courtyard below, Loch knew he'd met his match. The Mackinnon clan-chief had a cunning way about him, so different from Loch's father, who'd been all bluster and blunt-speech.

Mackinnon wasn't a man to trust, that much was clear.

"I didn't know yer father had died, at that point," Kendric Mackinnon replied after a lengthy pause. "As ye know, relations were ... strained ... between us."

Loch raised an incredulous eyebrow. Strained? Hostile more like. "And how do ye think we will put all of the bad blood behind us?"

"In the oldest way ... by bonding our two families through marriage." Mackinnon glanced in Tara's direction, his brow furrowing for an instant. "Unfortunately, my daughter is promised to someone else, or I would have offered ye her hand." He glanced back at Loch, his expression keen. "However, my brother has a comely daughter of marriageable age. She would be a fine match for ye."

"I can find myself a wife without yer assistance, Mackinnon," Loch replied, irritation spiking at the man's audacity. "Is that all ye are offering?"

The clan-chief shook his head. "I can offer ye *another* marriage alliance" —Mackinnon paused then, favoring Loch with a thin smile— "One between myself and yer sister."

Silence fell in the great hall.

Since seating himself at the long trestle table, Mackinnon hadn't looked Astrid's way, yet he did now—naked interest in his eyes. "I'd heard ye were a beauty, Lady Astrid," he murmured, "and I'm pleased to see that the tales have not been exaggerated."

Astrid stared back at him, her lovely face stony.

Recovering from his surprise, Loch cleared his throat. "I'd have thought ye would have tried to arrange a match between yer *son* and my sister ... rather than claim her for yerself."

Mackinnon's son frowned at this, while the clan-chief smirked. "Bran can't even grow whiskers properly upon his chin" —the lad flushed red at this, yet his father continued, oblivious to his son's embarrassment— "He isn't yet old enough to take a wife ... while *I* have been recently widowed." His gaze bored into Loch. "It would be an excellent choice for yer sister ... for word is that she's willful and could do with a firm hand."

Loch took another sip of wine, letting silence draw out again as he considered the offer.

In truth, he was conflicted.

Mackinnon wasn't wrong about Astrid. She was a spitfire all right. He grew tired of her undermining him at every turn. Loch had told himself that he was soon going to have to make her position in the castle clear, once and for all—yet Mackinnon had just handed him a way to deal with her.

However, she was his sister—the only close kin he had left. If he gave Astrid to Mackinnon, he'd never build a relationship with her again.

Loch's gaze went to Astrid then. The blood had drained from her face, and the knuckles of her hand that clenched her untouched goblet of wine had turned white. But, to his surprise, she held her tongue.

He'd expected another of the fiery whips of temper that she'd unleashed upon him over the past two weeks, but none was forthcoming. His sister had some sense of propriety, at least.

The silence continued to stretch out, swelling now. Impatience flickered across Mackinnon's face although he wisely held his tongue.

"I might consider yer offer," Loch said after another lengthy pause.

13: BREAKING WITH THE OLD WAYS

ASTRID MADE A soft choking sound while, next to Loch, Finn shifted position, his boiled leather armor creaking. Jack breathed a curse then, although Loch cut him a warning glance.

He didn't want to use Astrid this way, yet his focus now had to be on making his clan strong, on working toward peace. He'd be a fool not to consider a marriage alliance, or to let family loyalty cloud his judgment.

"However," he continued, his gaze returning to the clan-chief. "It would come with conditions."

Mackinnon's expression veiled. "And what would they be?"

"That ye return the two dozen cattle yer clan has stolen from ours over the last year ... that ye tell yer fishermen to keep to their own waters ... and that ye move yer cottars from the shores of Faing Burn, north of Dounarwyse Castle." Loch paused then, letting his words settle. "That's *Maclean* land."

Kendric Mackinnon raised a dark-auburn eyebrow. "Is it? Amongst my people ... that burn has always belonged to the Mackinnons." His mouth twisted then. "I'll ensure the local fishermen don't stray too far south. However, ye have no proof that my clan has stolen yer cattle. There's a group of MacDonald cattle rustlers at large, at present. It could well have been them."

Loch's jaw hardened. "The thieves were spotted ... and they were wearing yer plaid. And *yer* warriors burned Maclean homes, raped women ... and drove those who didn't die defending their bothies off fields they have tended for generations." He stared the clan-chief down, anger igniting in his belly. At that moment, peace was the last thing he wanted. Like Jack, his soul sang for revenge, yet he tamped the instinct down. He'd just come from a decade of violence, and it had left a bitter taste in his mouth. "If ye want to wed my sister, those are my terms."

The Mackinnon glared back at him, annoyance sparking in his eyes. These negotiations weren't going as he'd hoped. "I'd heard Iain Maclean's whelp was a cocky upstart," he murmured, his tone cooling now. "But I assumed ye would be better to deal with than yer bull-headed father. I was mistaken."

Loch's mouth curved into a thin smile. This was a battle, not of swords, but words. He still had the upper hand, which was why his rival had turned nasty. "Ye can have yer alliance, Mackinnon," he replied. "Surely, the things I ask for aren't unreasonable?"

Loch was aware then that Astrid was watching him. Anger still burned in her eyes—ire directed at him rather than Mackinnon.

It must be done, he told himself firmly, refusing to allow guilt to soften his stance. *Astrid is a clan-chief's daughter; she knows that with privilege comes responsibility.*

A clan-chief had to rule with his head, not his heart—and that meant making unpopular decisions when necessary. If he wished to wed Astrid to his rival to restore peace, he would. She would have to submit.

Another heavy pause followed, tension rippling across the great hall.

Kendric Mackinnon scowled, while his son and daughter looked on, both their expressions strained. Their gazes then flicked between their father and Loch. Unlike the Mackinnon, they'd been uncomfortable the moment they'd dismounted their horses in the outer courtyard.

They were in enemy territory here and no doubt worried their father would get all of them into trouble.

But Mackinnon was too wily for that.

As the moments passed, the anger in his eyes dimmed, replaced with an expression of quiet cunning. "Ye drive a hard bargain, Maclean," he said finally, "... but for the sake of peace, I shall overlook the slights ye have accused me of." His gaze flicked once more to Astrid, who sat frozen in her seat. His lips lifted at the corners. "I concede."

"Ye have betrayed me!"

Astrid didn't even wait until they were alone before she turned on him.

The Mackinnons had departed the great hall, accompanied by servants who'd take them to their lodgings. Highland hospitality dictated that they let them stay overnight.

Pursing his lips, Loch pushed himself to his feet. "Enough, Astrid," he growled.

Face flushed, she leaped up and stalked around the table toward him, elbowing Finn out of the way when he tried to stop her. "I have a say in my future, brother."

"Up to a certain point, aye," he replied turning to face her. Maybe Mackinnon was right—what she needed was a firm hand. "But ye know as well as I that when peace is at stake, ye need to heed yer clan-chief."

Astrid balled her hands into fists at her sides. She looked as if she wanted to strike him. "Ye can't force me to wed that man. I. Will. Not."

Loch scowled. It was bad enough that his sister defied him when they were alone, but he didn't like her embarrassing him in front of Jack and Finn. "Ye *will*, lass," Loch replied, stubbornness kicking in now. "If Mackinnon keeps to his side of the agreement, I will make sure of it."

“I can’t believe ye’d do this, Loch,” Jack spoke up then, his voice low and hard. “That ye’d wed Astrid to ‘The Butcher of Dun Ara’.”

Loch cut his cousin a warning look. “Keep out of this.” Jack’s opinion couldn’t be trusted when it came to the Mackinnons. Aye, he knew Kendric’s moniker—the name he’d earned himself over the years after the bloody campaigns he’d waged against his enemies—he didn’t need reminding of it.

“Ye can’t be thinking about making peace with him?” Jack countered, anger twisting his face. “Kendric Mackinnon has my father’s blood on his hands ... and no amount of peace-weaving will ever scrub them clean.”

“Ye’re letting hate blind ye, Jack,” Finn muttered. “Loch knows what he’s doing. A laird sometimes must make unpopular choices, for the good of his clan.”

“Shut yer gob, MacDonald,” Astrid snarled, her eyes narrowing into slits as she turned her fury upon him. Finn glared back, undaunted, yet she’d already shifted her attention back to Loch. “What ye should have done today was state yer terms and send Mackinnon away like the cur he is. Offering me up makes ye look weak.”

Heat ignited in Loch’s gut. Once again, his sister was undermining him, and he wouldn’t tolerate it. “Yer opinion wasn’t asked for, Astrid,” he replied, his voice roughening.

“No, but I shall voice it anyway. And if Da were here, he’d agree with me.”

Loch scowled. “He was too stubborn. It’s time we broke from the old ways.”

“Da was ten times the man ye are.” Astrid spat out the words, each one landing like a deftly thrown knife. “He also had age and experience behind him, and he’d never—”

“Enough!” Loch roared, cutting her off mid-tirade. He’d not weather any more of his sister’s insults. Stepping forward, he placed heavy hands on Astrid’s slim shoulders. She tried to twist away, but he held her fast.

Astrid glared up at him, her eyes glittering, and her fury and venom hit him like a battering ram to the breastbone.

Loch's pulse thudded. He never thought one of his kin would ever look on him like that, least of all the little sister who'd once worshipped him.

There was no sign of that loving lass he'd once taken for granted now though. It was like looking into the face of a stranger—and although there was a part of him that wanted to lay the blame at her feet, he couldn't. This was *his* doing.

Mairi was walking through the twice-weekly market upon the dock at Craignure, wicker basket under one arm, when she spied Loch amongst the crowd. He was talking to the ferryman, who'd depart shortly for the mainland. A single-masted birlinn was moored a few yards down the jetty, bobbing with the tide.

Her step faltered, and she came to a halt. An instant later, despite the cold and dampness of the day, heat washed over her.

Christ's teeth, what is he doing here?

She was about to turn back then, to leave her shopping for another day, when the laird's dark gaze snapped her way, pinning her to the spot.

He then nodded to the ferryman and stepped away, heading through the press of men and women who jostled around stalls of produce, cheeses, eggs, and freshly butchered meat toward her.

Seabirds screeched and wheeled overhead, no doubt eyeing the market for scraps. Meanwhile, a few yards away, fishermen hauled in their boats onto the white-sand beach. A crowd of women was gathering there too, waiting to buy the best of the day's catch.

However, Mairi's focus wasn't on the fishermen, the shouts of the vendors on the docks, or the local women who bustled by. Instead, she watched Loch's approach.

Noting the determination in his long strides, her belly fluttered. Why, after all this time, did the mere sight of the man make her feel as if her insides were melting? The closer he drew, the shallower her breathing became, and by the time he stopped in front of her, she felt dangerously light-headed.

"Good day, Mairi," he greeted her, a smile curving his lips.

"Loch," she replied, clearing her throat as her voice grew traitorously husky. Her gaze then roamed over his face. His lip had healed, and his black eye had faded—only a slight bruise at the inner edge remained. "Ye are certainly looking prettier than the last time I saw ye."

His smile widened, and the melting sensation inside her intensified. "Aye, the goatweed did the trick with the eye."

"I'm glad to hear it."

He took a step closer then, his gaze searching. "How have ye been?"

Mairi's traitorous heart skipped a beat. "Well enough."

"Ye haven't had any more trouble?"

She shook her head. Nearly a fortnight had passed since the brawl, and things had been quiet in the aftermath. "Ramsay MacDonald and his friends haven't shown their faces again since," she replied.

His smile developed a hard edge. "They won't either. After five days in the stocks, I had them run off my lands."

Mairi stiffened, taken aback by the brutality of his actions. She shouldn't have been surprised though. Loch wasn't a man to cross. His dark gaze grew intense then. "I won't have anyone disrespect ye like that, Mairi."

The low timbre of his voice, and the force behind it, made her suppress a shiver.

She wasn't sure how to respond to such a statement—and the unconscious irony of it wasn't lost on her. Hadn't he disrespected her recently, by turning up at the inn and expecting her to welcome him back to her bed as if no time had passed?

Aye, the man had a nerve, and she should tell him so.

And yet, part of her—the foolish part that still longed for him—thrilled to hear those words.

14: THE GODDESS

AN AWKWARD PAUSE followed before Mairi eventually broke it. "And ye, Loch?" she asked huskily. "How are things at Duart?"

A groove appeared between his eyebrows, and his mouth pursed.

Mairi inclined her head. "That bad?"

"Just the usual matters that a laird has to deal with." He pulled a face then. "Although it doesn't help that my sister now thinks I'm Satan."

Mairi raised her eyebrows. She wasn't surprised the two of them had locked horns, although she was taken aback that he'd admit such to her. "Ye aren't trying to clip her wings, are ye?" she teased lightly.

He snorted, hesitating then, as if debating whether to confide in her. "I'm in the process of trying to make peace with the Mackinnons ... and part of that is a marriage alliance."

Mairi's ribs constricted at this admission. An instant later, she inwardly kicked herself. *Goose. Of course, he'll take a wife. Why are ye surprised?*

"Kendric Mackinnon is recently widowed," Loch continued, oblivious to her reaction. "And he's asked for Astrid's hand."

Mairi let out a sharp exhale, realizing she'd misunderstood him. It wasn't *Loch* who was getting married, but Astrid. A second later, shock rippled through her. Surely, he hadn't promised his sister to 'The Butcher of Dun Ara'? "And ye *agreed?*"

Irritation flickered across his face. "I did … on a few conditions." His features tightened then. "Although, as I said, Astrid now hates me."

"I'm not surprised." Mairi wouldn't want to be given to the Mackinnon either. However, that wasn't ever likely. She was an innkeeper's daughter, while Lady Astrid was sister to the Maclean clan-chief. "I would too in her place."

He favored her with a tight smile. "But ye do already, *don't ye*, Mairi?"

Heat swept over her once more. The devil take him, Loch always had to push things. She was tempted to tell him that indeed, she loathed him, that she'd spit on his grave when he died.

But they both knew that would be a lie.

And so, she held his gaze and spoke the truth. "I wish I did," she said softly. "Life would be much easier."

Loch's eyes widened at her response. Nearby, a fowl started squawking. The sound then cut off as the vendor snapped the hapless bird's neck.

After a few moments, Loch cleared his throat. "Samhuinn approaches. Will ye join the celebrations at Duart?"

Mairi tensed. She usually did. Every year, she and Alison donned their guises and joined the throng of locals who walked the coastal path to Duart Castle. There, on the headland, burned a great bonfire, and they spent the last evening of October welcoming the coming of winter and paying tribute to the dead.

But now that Loch had returned, she wasn't sure she'd attend.

He stepped closer to her then, his gaze ensnaring hers. Mairi breathed in his scent, and a wave of dizziness crashed over her once more.

"If I ask ye … will ye come?" he asked softly.

Mairi's breathing grew shallow. She should refuse, yet his nearness, the gentle imploration in his voice, made her weaken.

"Perhaps," she replied, hating herself.

Mairi's heart skipped another beat when a slow smile quirked his mouth and his cheek dimpled. "I will look out for ye then."

Heart pounding now, she stepped back from him, clutching her basket to her as if it were her lifeline. "I'd better get on," she said, cursing the way her voice caught. "The best produce will be all gone at this rate. I shouldn't linger, anyway. Alison will be expecting me back."

Loch nodded. "When ye return to the inn, tell Tor we'll be leaving shortly."

"Tor?"

"Aye, the lad went to get himself an ale while I was busy ... and he's lingering over it." His smile widened. "I'd wager he's forgotten me by now. He'll be too busy flirting with yer cousin."

As Mairi approached the inn—her basket full of carrots, onions, apples, and fresh eggs— she studied it with a critical eye.

The sign above the door was looking a bit weathered these days, and the thatch needed patching in places. However, *The Craignure Inn* was a solid building, a distinctive landmark in the village. Its whitewashed walls shone in the sun.

This morning, she didn't enter through the front door, as was her habit. Instead, she took the path that skirted the left of the building, leading to the stables that had been built onto the back of the inn.

Opposite them, the new wing was taking shape. Muir Maclean and his lads were hard at work at this hour, building the stone walls that would make up the shell of the addition.

Catching sight of Mairi, Muir flashed her a grin. "Morning!"

Drawing near, her attention shifted to the slowly rising walls. "Will ye have enough stone?" she asked, her brow furrowing.

Muir scratched his chin. "I thought we would have ... but we might run out."

Mairi gave a brisk nod. "Let me know if ye have to make another trip to the quarry, and I shall give ye the coin."

"Aye, thank ye, Mairi."

She caught a glint of respect in the older man's gaze then. Mairi was still finding her feet as the owner of this inn, and initially, Muir had patronized her a little. Yet, as the days went on, she grew in confidence.

Leaving Muir and his team to their work, she made her way inside. And when she entered the common room, she found Tor leaning up against the bench, chatting to Alison.

The inn wasn't busy at this hour, and as such, her cousin was focused on him rather than her chores.

They both looked Mairi's way as she entered.

Aye, Loch had the right of it—the pair of them had been flirting. Alison had a twinkle in her eye, while Tor's cheeks were flushed.

Mairi eyed them, amusement tugging at her. The lad had been so shy on his last visit here that he'd hardly been able to meet her eye—yet here he was, talking to Alison. And interestingly, her cousin seemed to be enjoying his company.

Alison was a contradiction. She was confident, with a breezy way about her that drew men in, but after her leannan—a husky fisherman from the south of the island—left her a year earlier, she'd become wary around men. Her cousin had wept for days after he'd announced he was marrying someone else, and she'd sworn she'd never trust men again. But, fortunately, Alison wasn't like Mairi. She didn't hold hurts to her breast. She was one of those people who always looked forward.

All the same, this was the first time in a long while that Mairi had seen Alison let her guard down in a man's company. She was only a couple of years older than Tor, yet there was a worldliness about Alison that the lad lacked, despite that he'd likely traveled and experienced more than she had.

"Loch is looking for ye, Tor," she greeted the lad. "He's ready to leave."

The lad jolted, hurriedly putting down his tankard and rising to his feet. He was tall and lanky, and towered over Alison. Favoring the lass with a lopsided smile, he then gave an awkward bow. "Shall I see ye at Samhuinn?"

"Aye, ye shall," Alison replied with an answering smile. "Now get on with ye, or the laird shall lose his patience."

Tor left with a shy duck of his head, covering the floor in long strides, and ducking through the low doorway. After he departed, the door thudding shut behind him, Mairi turned to Alison, her mouth curving. "It looks as if ye have an admirer there."

Her cousin shrugged. "Tor is charming."

"Aye ... which is more than can be said for a lot of the men around here."

Alison flashed Mairi a knowing smile before eyeing the basket she carried. "Ye ran into the laird at market then?"

Mairi nodded before moving past her cousin toward the kitchen. The morning was drawing out, and she had to get the mutton stew on for the evening and bake some apple cakes. However, Alison wasn't letting her get away so easily.

She hurried after Mairi, cornering her as she placed the basket on the kitchen table. "And?"

Mairi scowled. "And what?"

Alison gave her a quizzical look. "I thought ye two had mended things ... after the night of the brawl."

"No," Mairi replied brusquely. Her gaze narrowed then, even as Alison raised an incredulous eyebrow. They hadn't discussed Loch of late, yet her cousin missed little. "Not that there was anything to mend, anyway, Ali ... our past is dead and buried."

Loud mooing drew Mairi out of the inn.

Wiping her hands on her apron, for she'd been scrubbing tables, she stood on the doorstep and watched the large herd of stocky black cattle with long horns and shaggy coats thunder past.

"Those must be the missing cattle everyone's been talking about," Alison said, raising her voice to be heard over the din as she stepped up behind her.

"Aye," Mairi replied, eyeing the drovers upon ponies who brought up the rear of the group. The agreement their laird had made with his rival was the talk of the village these days. The drovers had sour expressions and wore clan sashes of blocky green and red plaid across their fronts. She wondered if Kendric Mackinnon was making a statement, delivering the missing livestock on the eve of Samhuinn.

The folk of Craignure had all ventured out of their bothies and gardens to watch the spectacle. Some of them jeered at the Mackinnons as they rode by, while others smiled excitedly.

"The laird did it!" the miller's wife, who stood with her friend a few feet away from Mairi, gasped. "He got our cattle back."

"Aye, and thanks to him, the Mackinnons have ceased fishing our waters," her companion replied. The two women, both carrying shopping baskets, had stopped to watch the passing cattle.

Mairi marked the approval in both their voices. Upon Loch's return, the locals had been wary of him. No doubt, they remembered the wild lad he'd once been and worried he'd make a poor laird. However, his actions since stepping into his father's role had reassured them.

For her part, Mairi cast a jaundiced eye upon the drovers. Even though they were delivering what had been stolen, she didn't welcome the Mackinnons here. She was a Macquarie, yet she'd grown up amongst the Macleans and was loyal to them. She knew what Loch was trying to achieve but didn't see how a marriage alliance could erase three generations of bitterness between the clans or sweep away all the wrongs the Mackinnons had done.

"Poor Lady Astrid," Alison said then as the last of the livestock and riders passed by, heading south. "She'll be hoping Mackinnon does something to anger her brother ... something to make the laird change his mind."

"Aye, although that doesn't look likely."

"I wonder if she'll attend tonight's celebration," Alison mused. "She usually does ... but she might not be in the mood for revelry now."

"I wouldn't blame her."

A brief pause followed before Alison spoke once more. "Ye still haven't told me if ye are coming with me later. Are ye?"

Mairi cast her cousin a sidelong glance to see that Alison had pinned her with a piercing look that demanded an answer.

"I don't know," Mairi replied with a sigh. "I might stay home this year. I could do with a quiet night. It's been busy at the inn of late."

Alison put her hands on her hips. "What kind of answer is that?"

"An honest one."

"But ye love the fire festivals?"

Mairi did, although she was reluctant to see Loch again, especially since just the sight of him tied her belly in knots and scattered her wits to the four winds. She didn't trust herself around the man.

When she didn't answer, Alison frowned. "It's something we always do together."

"I know ... but ye can go alone this once."

Alison continued to observe her, disappointment darkening her gaze.

"What?" Mairi huffed, irritation spearing her.

"I've made ye a new guise ... I was hoping ye'd wear it this year."

Mairi stiffened, guilt tightening her belly. "When have ye had the time for that?"

"In the evenings, after I finish work for the day ... I've been working on it for weeks."

The guilt wound tighter. "Oh, Ali," she murmured. "Ye shouldn't have."

"Why not?" A groove etched between Alison's eyebrows. "Ye have made guises for me over the years ... I wanted to do the same for ye."

Defeated, Mairi's shoulders slumped. "Very well," she said. "Let me see it."

Mairi surveyed her reflection in the looking glass. It was a small rectangular glass, one that her father had bought from a trader years earlier, especially for her—a gift she had treasured.

But this afternoon, she hardly recognized the woman before her.

"I look ... frightening," she said eventually, awed by the warrior queen staring back at her: the Morrígan, goddess of death, destiny, and battle.

Alison chuckled. "I did a good job then?"

"Aye." Mairi reached up, touching the crown of wood and black feathers that Alison had made for her. She wore a low-cut charcoal gown also made by her cousin's hand, cinched at the waist with a heavy leather belt—but the most splendid aspect of the guise was the cloak of inky-black feathers that hung from her shoulders. "How did ye find all these feathers?"

"As I said, I've been working on this for months," Alison replied, pride lacing her voice. "I've been collecting crow, raven, and blackbird feathers ... and then I bought a bag of them at market last month." She paused, stepping back to admire her handiwork. "Spin around for me."

Sighing, Mairi moved back from the looking glass and did as bid. The cloak flew out, sweeping around her as if she were a great crow.

Alison laughed and clapped her hands together in delight. She then moved toward the door. "Wait here ... I've got one final thing for ye."

Mairi did as bid, stealing another glance at herself in the looking glass.

She still didn't recognize herself. The Morrígan was dark-haired, like her, but the queen, who was said to be able to foresee death, was formidable, dangerous.

Wearing such a guise made Mairi straighten her spine and square her shoulders.

She was still gazing at her reflection when Alison returned, carrying a wooden staff with a carved crow's head. "I had Jamie the carpenter make this for ye," she said excitedly.

"This is too much," Mairi breathed, even as she took the staff from her cousin. "Have ye spent all yer savings?"

Alison snorted. "Of course not." She winked at Mairi then. "Ye know that Jamie's sweet on me."

Mairi stiffened. "But he's married."

"Aye, but that doesn't stop him from being an incorrigible flirt." Alison flashed her a coy smile. "All it took was a few smiles and sighs ... and he was happy to make the staff for a penny."

15: JUST A COINCIDENCE

"I CAN SEE the bonfire already ... look!"

Alison pointed south to where a glow illuminated the darkening sky.

"Aye, and they're playing music too," Mairi added, her mouth curving.

Indeed, the haunting strains of a highland pipe echoed over the cliffs, welcoming the two women as they walked toward Duart Castle.

The fortress itself had been visible for a while, a sentinel that crouched high over the headland, looking out to sea.

Mairi didn't walk this way often, for she was leashed to the inn these days, but the sight of Duart Castle never failed to take her breath away.

How does Loch feel ... to rule such a place? she wondered before kicking herself. How easily her thoughts strayed to him these days. Her mind hardly needed an excuse before seizing on the man.

To distract herself, Mairi glanced over at where Alison walked, her long skirts rustling. Her cousin had done a fine job of her own guise too; she was dressed as a water sprite, in a silvery kirtle and a headdress made of shells and seagull feathers. She'd even fashioned a pair of wings out of thin linen stretched over wicker.

Catching her eye, Alison grinned. "We look quite a pair tonight, cousin."

Mairi smiled back, although she inwardly cringed.

Curse Loch for asking me to attend, she thought bitterly. *And curse me too for agreeing to come.*

This wasn't how she'd planned to spend her evening. The inn was closed for Samhuinn, and it would have been a luxury indeed to put her feet up by the hearth in her bedchamber and enjoy a cup of mulled wine and a left-over apple cake. She certainly didn't want to be on her way to Duart dressed in her most eye-catching guise ever.

Already on the walk out of Craignure, she'd caught men staring at her, their gazes lingering on the low-cut bodice of her gown.

Glancing down at it now, she frowned. "God's teeth, Alison ... this dress is almost indecent," she muttered. Indeed, the dress thrust her full breasts up and emphasized the deep cleavage between them. She grabbed the bodice then and attempted to hike it higher.

"Nonsense," Alison replied indignantly. "It's just showing yer paps off a little, that's all."

Mairi snorted. "A little? I won't be dancing in this guise, I can tell ye ... or they'll break lose and smash my nose flat."

Alison hooted with laughter, the merry sound echoing along the cliffs, and causing the group of revelers walking ahead of them—a family, all dressed up as wulvers, selkies, and broonies—to twist around and stare at them.

Ignoring the attention she was attracting, Alison linked her arm through Mairi's and squeezed tight. "This will be a Samhuinn to remember; I can feel it."

Mairi didn't reply. She looked down at her paps again and pulled a face. *Hopefully, not for the wrong reasons.*

The cousins walked on, and after a short while, Alison squeezed Mairi's arm once more. "Have ye ever thought about taking a husband?"

Stiffening, Mairi cut her an arch look. "Where did that question come from?"

A groove appeared between Alison's eyebrows. "Ye work hard ... and are more than capable of running the inn on yer own. But wouldn't ye be happier if ye had a loving man at yer side ... if ye had someone to shoulder the burden with?"

Mairi snorted. "I don't see the inn as a burden ... and anyway, I've got *ye*, Ali."

A pause followed before Alison replied, "That's not what I meant." The line between her eyebrows deepened. "Isn't it time to let the past go?"

Tension rippled through Mairi at these words. She knew what her cousin was implying.

Isn't it time to let Loch go?

Aye, she understood what Alison was getting at, yet she didn't want to admit that, even after all these years, there was a part of her that clung to the memory of what she'd once shared with Loch Maclean.

"A husband is the last thing I need," she said firmly, squeezing Alison's arm back. "However, ye and I could do with assistance on busy evenings. I need to look into hiring extra help."

"Who are ye supposed to be?" Finn eyed Loch as he descended the steps from the keep into the inner courtyard.

Loch pulled a face. "Isn't it obvious?" He was shirtless this eve, his chest painted with black Celtic swirls, while about his shoulders, he wore a hooded cloak. A horned headdress and a large wooden club completed the guise.

Finn shook his head. He was clad in furs with a pair of antlers strapped to his head. "No ... enlighten me."

"Idiot," Jack replied, stepping up behind Finn. "Anyone can see he's The Dagda ... the warrior god." His cousin's tone was dry although not terse this evening.

Relations between Loch and Jack had been strained ever since Loch had struck a bargain with the Mackinnon. They got along well enough, as long as no one brought up the topic, and it seemed that tonight, his cousin had decided to put his resentment aside.

Finn turned to Jack then, favoring him with a wry smile. "The Headless Horseman of Mull rides again, I see."

Jack pulled a face. "I thought I'd have ye all guessing."

Loch eyed his cousin's macabre guise. Jack's face peeked out from within the voluminous black cloak he wore. He'd used a frame of sticks underneath the mantle to create the illusion of a pair of shoulders above his head, where a round log, tipped with red to resemble the bloodied stump of a neck, protruded.

He then slapped Jack on the shoulder. "Come on … let's get some mulled wine."

"Aye," Jack muttered as they set off across the courtyard. "I could do with a barrel of it."

Loch's mouth pursed. As could he. The afternoon had been a trying one. After the excitement of the arrival of the missing cattle earlier in the day, Astrid had flown into a rage. She'd been so incensed that she'd threatened to throw herself off the walls onto the rocks if he didn't break his proposed alliance with the Mackinnon.

Her reaction had been disconcerting, yet Loch hadn't backed down. He wouldn't let his sister blackmail him. Unsurprisingly, Astrid had refused to attend the Samhuinn festivities. This evening, he'd left his sister in the ladies' solar with her maid for company.

Wordlessly, the three men made their way outside into the gloaming. Walking down the road that led away from the gates, Loch's gaze traveled west to where the sunset burnished the long, sculpted edge of Dùn da Ghaoithe.

His mouth curved at the sight of the mountain. All those years away, he'd missed this view.

Of late, Dùn da Ghaoithe had often been obscured, and Loch hadn't managed another ride up its scree-covered slopes. Wind and rain had battered Mull over the past weeks, isolating them from the mainland. The bad weather often delayed the ferry between Oban and Craignure, prevented the fisherman from going out, and drove the shepherds off the nearby hills.

It was a rare fine evening, and he wished to enjoy it.

The rich scent of woodsmoke laced the air, as did the aroma of chestnuts roasting. Braziers glowed on the hillside, beneath the great fire that illuminated the twilight like a beacon. A troupe of pipers was playing a jaunty tune, and children were already dancing, their happy squeals echoing high into the sky.

Loch surveyed it all, and a kernel of warmth germinated within him.

These were his people. His clan. This isle was where he truly belonged.

It had been a long time since he'd attended Samhuinn festivities. Over the past years, the military campaigning had absorbed all his attention. Sometimes it seemed as if the decade had passed in the blink of his eye. War had a way of both slowing time down and speeding it up. The endless winters, up to his knees in mud, had gone on forever. And then, suddenly, it was all over. The English had been defeated—and it was time to go home.

"Look at that." Jack's low, appreciative whistle intruded then. "It seems The Morrígan has come in search of her lover." He then nudged Loch with his elbow. "Get ready ... ye lucky devil."

Irritated at the intrusion on his thoughts, Loch glanced away from the bonfire, his gaze traveling to where a statuesque woman clad in a revealing charcoal-colored gown glided through the crowd. She was a beauty with long dark hair and proud carriage. A cloak of black feathers rippled from her shoulders, and she carried a staff with a crow perched atop it.

Loch stared, momentarily transfixed.

A heartbeat later, his breathing caught as he recognized her.

"Lord, Alison, what have ye done?" Mairi came to an abrupt halt, her heart leaping into her throat.

"What?" Alison glanced her way, her golden-brown eyes snapping wide.

Mairi glared back at her. "Take a look ahead," she said, her voice strangled now. "At the laird."

Her cousin did as bid, her gaze traveling across the crowd of revelers, most of them guised for Samhuinn, to where a tall dark-haired man stood. He was cloaked, with a horned crown upon his head. On his lower half, he wore tight-fitting leather breeches, while his muscular chest was bare and painted in Celtic swirls—and in one hand, he carried a heavy wooden club.

Loch looked darkly handsome and dangerous tonight, but that wasn't the problem—his *guise* was.

Alison stared at him a moment before realization dawned. She then breathed an oath before murmuring. "The Dagda."

"Aye, and do ye remember yer folklore?"

Her cousin dragged her attention from Loch to meet her eye once more. She then favored Mairi with a sheepish smile. "The Morrígan and The Dagda were lovers."

"Aye ... and do ye recall what was supposed to happen between them at Samhuinn?"

Alison gave her a blank look, and Mairi made an exasperated sound in the back of her throat. She felt like grabbing her cousin by the shoulders and giving her a shake. "They *coupled*," she bit out.

Alison's eyes widened once more before she gave her head a rueful shake. "Don't look so panicked, cousin ... it's merely folklore. No one expects ye to drag the laird away and give him a good—"

"*He* might though," Mairi snapped, cutting her off. "There's no bounds to that man's nerve."

Her cousin sighed then, placing a placating hand on Mairi's arm. "I had no idea Loch would come guised as The Dagda, I swear. As I said ... I'd been working on yer guise for the past few months." There was a note of hurt in Alison's voice now, and Mairi suddenly felt ashamed of herself.

Of course, Alison hadn't known. It was just ill fortune.

Her attention shifted across the crowd to where Loch stood, flanked by Jack and Finn. The laird had seen her, and he was watching Mairi with a slightly stunned look upon his face, as if he couldn't quite believe his eyes either.

A moment later, he stepped away from his companions' side and wove his way through the crowd toward her.

Mairi swallowed hard. *Christ's bones, no!*

She broke his stare, cutting a glare at her cousin. However, Alison had moved off, calling out to one of her friends, who was ladling out cups of mulled wine.

Mairi now stood alone.

Silently cursing Alison, Mairi shifted her attention back to Loch. Moments later, he was standing in front of her.

Their gazes fused before his mouth lifted at the corners. “Ye came.”

Mairi cleared her throat. “Aye.” How she wished she hadn’t. How she wanted to be at home, avoiding this awkwardness.

His gaze raked over her, traveling from the wooden crown upon her head, down her body.

Heat washed over Mairi. His look stripped her naked, and her palm itched to slap him for his audacity. “That’s a fetching guise,” he murmured finally.

“Aye, well … when I heard ye were coming as The Dagda, I thought I’d better don a guise worthy of ye,” she replied, feigning a flippancy she didn’t feel.

His eyes darkened. He then stepped close, too close, his head lowering so that when he spoke once more, his breath tickled her ear. “That’s daring of ye, Mairi … especially since ye know what The Morrígan and her lover get up to on Samhuinn.”

Mairi took a brisk step back, deliberately creating space between them. “My guise is a gift from my cousin,” she declared, deciding to end the game they were playing. “She’s been working on it for months.” She reached up, her fingers stroking the feather cloak that covered her shoulders. “I’ve never had anyone make such an effort on my behalf.”

She raised her chin then, her gaze meeting Loch’s once more. In truth, he was even more distracting than usual tonight, with his chest bared and those tight leather breeches. It was impossible to ignore the hard-muscled lines of his chest, covered with whorls of crisp dark hair, or the way the leather cupped the swell of his groin.

His expression was shuttered now though, and she was relieved. Her response had made it clear that she wasn’t here to flirt with him. She didn't intend to spend much time with Loch at all.

"Indeed, it's a coincidence that we came guised as we have," she pointed out then, eager to draw a line between them.

Loch's mouth quirked, his night-brown eyes gleaming. "Is it a coincidence, mo leannan," he murmured, "or fate?"

Mairi tensed. Loch was up to his old tricks, trying to spin a web of enchantment around her. But she wouldn't be drawn in. She wasn't eighteen and gullible. She wouldn't have her heart broken again.

"I don't believe in fate," she replied, moving past him.

16: INTO THE NIGHT

LOCH WATCHED MAIRI walk away. Her black cloak rippled behind her, highlighting her proud bearing.

It was difficult not to stare.

Mairi Macquarie might have been born an innkeeper's daughter, yet tonight, she carried herself like a warrior queen. Dressing as The Morrígan had made her fiercer than usual, yet he'd enjoyed the way she responded to him.

It was a strange coincidence that they'd unwittingly dressed as lovers, although that didn't matter. What did was the sight of her quickened his blood and tightened his belly. He was glad that she'd attended Samhuinn, for he'd thought she wouldn't.

And once her temper cooled, he'd approach her again.

Wandering back through the crowd, Loch helped himself to some mulled wine along the way, although he turned down the offer of soul cakes.

There was only one thing he was hungry for at present, and it wasn't food.

Eventually, he found his way back to where Jack and Finn stood. Both men held cups of mulled wine, steam rising into the crisp night air. Finn was smiling as he watched a group of local lasses, dressed as fairies, skipping around the fire.

Finn's smile widened as Loch joined them. "Looks like it'll be a merry eve."

Loch grinned back. "Aye … it *will* be."

It was one of the liveliest Samhuinn fires that Mairi had ever attended, yet she spent most of it avoiding Loch.

Wherever she was, and whomever she was talking to, she kept one wary eye out for The Dagda's approach. Fortunately, he let her be.

Many of those attending the celebrations—young and old alike—danced around the fire. However, Mairi didn't. She'd meant what she'd said to Alison earlier: the dress was so low cut that she was in constant peril of spilling out of it.

As the hours wore on, she grew tired of men talking to her chest rather than her face. She also grew tired of listening to gossips. Spirits were high tonight after the return of the missing cattle. A group of local drovers danced with their wives a few yards from where Mairi stood, grins upon their faces.

She watched their merriment yet had no desire to join the dancing anyway. The two cups of wine she'd drunk had relaxed her, and she'd just started on her third, but Mairi felt as if she were on the outside looking in this evening. And even though there was no shortage of people to talk to and catch up with, sadness stole upon her.

The Samhuinn past, the three of them—her, Alison, and Athol—had walked here together. As usual, her father had been at the heart of everything, drinking heavily and dancing with local women. Mairi had often wondered why he'd never wed again after her mother died. Once, at an unguarded moment, he'd told Mairi that her mother was the love of his life; he'd known the moment he set eyes on her that there would be no other woman for him. That didn't stop him from socializing at fire festivals though or flirting with widows.

Mairi's throat thickened. How she missed the rumble of his voice and the deep boom of his laughter.

Taking another sip of mulled wine, her gaze slid over the dancers, to where Alison skipped about the fire, hand in hand with Tor.

The young warrior looked striking this eve. He wore a wolfskin, with the head intact, draped over his head and shoulders. Both his and Alison's faces were flushed with cold, wine, and exertion—and they were laughing as they spun around together.

Mairi watched them, an arrow of envy lancing through her chest. How she wished to feel that carefree again.

Stifling a sigh, she shifted her attention from her cousin, across the crowd of revelers, to where Loch was deep in conversation with Jack. The laird's cousin had guised himself as The Headless Horseman of Mull.

Mairi glanced away, noting that, for the first time all evening, no one was taking any notice of her.

It was the right moment to leave.

Draining the last of her wine, she dropped the empty cup into a nearby wicker basket before wending her way around the outskirts of the revelry.

Nearby, next to the road that led north through Duart village and then on to Craignure, a row of torches had been lit. They were essential, for despite the full moon, it would be dangerous to travel so close to the cliffs without something to light the way.

Mairi looked over her shoulder then, her gaze traveling to Loch once more.

He was still talking to Jack.

She knew she shouldn't let her gaze linger on him—if he saw her, it would only encourage him—yet she couldn't help it.

Her heart jolted then as another realization struck her. She still loved him, and curse her, she always would. Mairi had inherited her father's loyalty it seemed. Once she gave her heart away, there was no taking it back.

Throat tight and eyes burning, she turned and helped herself to a torch. Then, she set off toward Craignure.

"Samhuinn always reminds me of my Da." Jack's fern-green eyes were glazed with wine and memories as he stared at the dancing flames of the bonfire. "Every year, he'd dress as a druid of old ... donning a black cloak and wreathing mistletoe through his hair."

Loch's mouth curved. "My father usually guised himself as the Holly King."

Memories filtered back then, of Iain Maclean striding through the crowd in a voluminous robe. He'd been quite a sight with his dark-golden hair unbound, a crown of holly around his head, and a big grin on his face. He'd always had a big cup of mulled wine in one hand and a soul cake in the other. His father had a loud voice and a deep rumbling laugh that carried over the crowd.

Loch had loved that guise as a bairn; yet once he grew up, he'd found it ridiculous. And he'd told his father so.

"I still miss him, ye know."

Jack's admission, spoken barely louder than a whisper, caught Loch by surprise. His cousin had been in high spirits earlier, yet his mood had changed as the night drew out. Jack had always been more emotional than Loch, and drink tended to bring his feelings to the surface. "Ye rarely speak of yer father," he pointed out after a pause.

His cousin glanced his way, his proud face strained. "That's because it drags up too many memories." Jack's mouth twisted then. "Maybe I shouldn't have come back to Mull."

Loch cocked an eyebrow. "It's yer home."

Jack shook his head, his gaze shadowing. "I felt like a stranger at Dounarwyse."

"That's hardly surprising ... ye hate yer brother."

Jack snorted. "Aye, but it's more than that ... everywhere I turn, the shadows of the past taunt me. Sometimes I think I'd have been better off making a fresh start somewhere new." He paused then, his features tightening. "Ever since I stepped back on Mull, all I can think about is sticking a dirk in Kendric Mackinnon's throat. It's like a sickness, Loch ... and I can't seem to shake myself free of it."

Loch frowned as he considered this admission. He agreed, Jack hadn't been himself of late. However, he wasn't sure that leaving was the answer. Reaching out, he placed a hand on Jack's shoulder. "Just remember that Duart still welcomes ye."

Jack's lips lifted at the edges before he nodded. "I appreciate that ye made me yer marshal." He sighed then and dragged a hand down his face. "God's blood, I'm maudlin tonight. I need more wine." He nodded to Loch's cup. "Do ye want another?"

Loch shook his head. After the first cup of mulled wine, he'd drunk sparingly, for he wished to keep his senses sharp.

His brow furrowed once more as he watched Jack walk away. Sometimes his cousin worried him. Jack wore a devil-may-care air most of the time, yet he was someone who felt deeply—too deeply, at times.

Still mulling the things Jack had revealed, Loch let his gaze travel over the revelers. He was looking for Mairi, but he couldn't find her.

Her cousin was still dancing with Tor—those two had been inseparable all night—and Mairi had been standing on the fringe of the dancers looking on earlier.

But not now.

Loch had been planning to approach her again, once she'd mellowed, to ask her to dance. But his conversation with Jack had distracted him. His gaze narrowed now as he realized she'd managed to leave without him noticing—and that she'd headed off into the night. Alone.

Mairi walked briskly along the cliffs, torch held high in one hand, her crow staff in the other.

It was a bonnie night to be outdoors. Waves hissed against the rocks below, while behind her, the great Samhuinn bonfire illuminated the sky. Above, the huge silver moon hung like a brightly polished penny, frosting the folds of hills that rolled away to the east.

The isle was striking during the day with its wild coast and mountainous interior, yet illuminated by the cold light of the moon, it almost seemed otherworldly.

Mairi's skin prickled; one could almost imagine the Daoine Sìth, the fairy folk, were about on such a night.

The farther she walked from Duart, the more she relaxed. How rare it was to have such peace and solitude.

Mairi had little time to herself these days. Life at *The Craignure Inn* had always been busy, yet since her father's death, she sometimes felt like an overburdened ox pulling a plow. The only time she had alone with her thoughts was first thing in the morning and last thing at night when she retired to her bedchamber. The rest of the time, her mind was constantly running ahead, ensuring that the inn ran smoothly.

Lost in thought, she didn't hear someone calling her name at first.

It was only when the glow of another torch joined hers that Mairi swung around, her heart leaping into her throat.

"Mairi!"

She brought her staff up, ready to swing it at an attacker.

But then her gaze fell upon Loch Maclean's swarthy face. Cursing, she lowered the staff, her fingers clenched around the polished wood. "Christ's teeth," she muttered. "What are ye doing sneaking up on folk?"

He grinned at her, teeth flashing white against his short dark beard. "Looking for ye."

Her already pounding heart stuttered. "Why?"

Holding his torch aloft, he fell in next to her. "Ye shouldn't be walking home on yer own."

Mairi snorted. "I've done this journey alone plenty of times ... it's safe."

"During the day, aye ... but even upon this isle, ye should take care traveling without a man's protection at night."

Mairi wanted to dismiss his concern, yet she caught the edge to his voice. It wasn't a suggestion but a command.

Irritation swiftly followed. She didn't need him looking out for her. He wasn't her father or brother—or her husband for that matter. Clenching her jaw, she quickened her pace, wishing she were closer to Craignure.

Yet to her ire, Loch merely lengthened his long stride, easily keeping up with her.

The pair of them walked in silence, their feet scuffing on the dirt path that hugged the cliffs.

"Yer wellbeing does matter to me, Mairi," Loch said finally, breaking the quiet. "If ye believe nothing good about me … believe that."

Mairi was tempted to scoff at his assertion, yet his voice was quiet now, sincere.

She cut Loch a sidelong look. He was staring ahead, his profile sterner than usual.

"When ye first arrived back, I thought ye hadn't changed," she admitted after a pause. "But ye *are* different."

17: JUST ONE KISS

LOCH'S MOUTH LIFTED at the corners, and he glanced her way, their gazes meeting. "How so?"

"There's a maturity to ye these days."

His dark eyes glinted in the torchlight. "That's to be expected, lass ... I *am* older now."

Mairi gave a soft snort. "Age doesn't guarantee wisdom ... if it did, the world wouldn't be full of fools."

Loch laughed, the warm sound mingling with the rumble of the surf below.

"Leadership has been good for ye," Mairi added. "As has stepping into yer father's role."

"Perhaps," he replied, sobering. "Responsibility has a way of making ye focus on something other than yerself." He paused then. "For years, I had a company of warriors who relied on me ... and now a community of people looks to me for protection. I can't just think about myself anymore."

They'd reached the end of the cliffs now and were making their way down the hillside toward Craignure. The village crouched in shadow on the water's edge, moonlight sparkling off the gently lapping waves.

Loch and Mairi didn't speak for a short while. However, as they reached the bottom of the hill, he broke the weighty silence between them once more. "Ye are the only one I've ever let my guard down with, Mairi," he said, his voice lowering. "The only person who has ever understood me."

Mairi's breathing grew shallow, yearning twisting within her. She wished he wouldn't say such things.

"I'm sure yer family did," she replied, forcing a lightness she didn't feel into her voice. "Or would've, if ye'd given them a chance."

He gave a humorless laugh. "I didn't."

Mairi arched an eyebrow. "I remember that ye often clashed with yer Da."

"Aye … as soon as I was old enough, I made it my life's purpose to rebel, to be everything he wasn't."

"Why?"

Silence fell as Loch considered her question. "The old man could be an overbearing bastard at times," he said finally, his gaze fixed ahead. "He wouldn't leave me alone. He wanted me to be like him … to hold the same views, to make the same choices. I hated it."

His admission took Mairi aback. "I never spent any time with yer father," she replied after a few moments. "But to me, ye both seemed similarly pigheaded."

Loch snorted. "I suppose we were."

They were walking past the first of the bothies that lined the waterfront now. Soon enough, they'd reach the inn, and Mairi would bid Loch 'good night'. However, she found she didn't want to part from him yet. Their conversation had drawn her in, as had his revelations. Suddenly, she wanted to know more.

"Was that why ye never made a trip back here over the years?" she asked after a lengthy pause.

"Not really," he answered, with a grimace. "In truth, I was too focused on the war to spare my father much thought."

Mairi's belly tightened. *Or me?*

The question teetered on the tip of her tongue, yet she swallowed it. Loch was in a candid mood, and she might not like his reply.

Nonetheless, she was loath to sever the connection between them tonight. She liked feeling close to him again, being able to unlock his thoughts. "What was it like?" she asked after a pause. "Fighting for the Bruce."

Loch's mouth quirked. "Not as exciting as ye might think … there was a lot of waiting around … and a lot of mud."

"But ye fought in a few battles?"

"I did."

"And ye killed many men."

He nodded.

"Does it haunt ye?"

A pause followed as Loch considered her question. "Sometimes," he admitted. "In the beginning, I thought I'd never get used to killing ... but I did. And when ye become hardened to something like that, a piece of yer soul withers." Loch halted then, marshaling his thoughts, and when he continued, his voice was unusually subdued. "Maybe that's why I've committed myself to making peace with the Mackinnons now rather than fighting them. I've seen enough blood and guts, enough slaughter. I need to remind myself that life's about more than war ... that there's beauty and hope too."

Mairi's breathing grew shallow at these words. She hadn't suspected Loch felt that way. "There is," she assured him gently.

They passed the last few yards to the inn in silence. The building loomed before them, its whitewashed walls glowing pale silver, even in the darkness.

Stopping by the door, Mairi removed the heavy keys from her belt. Yet, instead of turning to unlock the door, she raised her chin and met Loch's gaze. He was watching her, his handsome face kissed by the moonlight.

A shiver went through her then; how she wanted him. Having Loch Maclean back in her life was both a delight and a torture. And his admission just now, his candidness, made her ache to reach out and touch him.

Step away, a voice whispered to her. But she didn't heed it.

"So, ye are happy to be home then?" she asked, holding his eye.

His mouth curved into a slow smile that made Mairi's heart kick against her ribs. "Aye," he murmured. "It's harder than I'd thought ... taking over the reins from my father and dealing with everything. But at the same time, it feels ... right."

Mairi smiled back. “I’m glad.” She toyed with the keys then, feeling their weight in her hand. “I’d better go … it’s late.”

He nodded.

She cleared her throat. “Very well.”

Their gazes held, and Loch’s expression grew serious. When he spoke once more, his voice held a husky note. “May I kiss ye goodnight, Mairi?”

Say no.

The voice was back, counseling her to be wary and wise.

She should have heeded it, should have stepped back and unlocked the door.

However, Mairi couldn’t move.

Instead, she found herself ensnared in the depths of Loch’s eyes. Need twisted sharply under her ribcage.

It had been so long—surely, just one kiss wouldn’t hurt?

Just one.

And so, she found herself nodding. She then wet her lips before whispering, “Aye.”

She’d expected Loch to smile, to flash her one of his arrogant, victorious grins at her acquiescence. But he didn’t. His expression remained serious, his eyes intent, as he stepped close. He then brushed a lock of hair off her cheek, his gaze roaming her face.

Mairi held her breath, anticipation quickening within her.

Slowly, he bowed his head. She was a tall woman, and so he didn’t have to stoop to kiss her.

When his lips brushed Mairi’s, her heart started fluttering like a caged bird. He raised his head then, his gaze finding hers once more as if he wanted to make sure she welcomed this.

Dear Lord, she did.

With a sigh, Mairi swayed toward him, her lips parting.

That was all the sign he needed as he leaned in again, his hands rising to cup her face—and then his mouth was on hers.

Loch's tongue swept her lips apart, and he tasted her. An instant later, he was exploring Mairi's mouth with slow, sensual deliberation that made all thought flee her mind. All she could care about, all she could focus on, was how good he tasted, and on the combined gentleness and strength in the hands that cupped her face.

The kiss went on, languorous and exploratory, as if he had all the time in the world.

But it couldn't last forever, and when Loch drew back, Mairi swallowed a cry of disappointment.

The Saints forgive her, she'd forgotten how good his kisses were. Every slide and flick of his tongue made her feel as if she were melting, like a tallow candle burned down to a stump.

She'd thought he'd deepen the kiss further, and slide his hands down from her face, to explore her body, but he didn't. Instead, Loch stepped back. He was breathing hard though, his bare chest rising and falling sharply.

"Goodnight, Mairi," he said roughly.

Mairi's belly swooped. She couldn't believe it. He really did intend to give her one kiss and be on his way.

However, the yearning inside her had gathered to a wild storm now—her need for him so strong that her body trembled.

And without questioning her behavior, or hardly realizing what she was doing, she reached out and caught his hand. "Don't go," she whispered.

His eyes widened.

Mairi gently squeezed his hand. "I mean it," she continued, even as her pulse thundered in her ears. "Stay."

A deep groan rumbled up from his throat, and he stepped close once more, gathered her into his arms, and kissed her again.

His first kiss and been slow and exploratory, yet this one was feverish, hot. He plundered her mouth with his tongue, yet Mairi responded just as hungrily. Standing on the doorstep of the inn, their bodies pressed flush, they forgot about where they were.

Even through their clothing, Mairi could feel his arousal, pressing like a wooden baton against her stomach. Dizziness assailed her as the kiss deepened further, and when Loch's hands traveled down the curve of her back and cupped her backside, squeezing gently, she moaned into his mouth.

Breathing hard, he broke off the kiss, burying his face in her neck.

"God's blood," he growled. "We need to go inside, lass ... before I take ye up against the wall."

She gave a shaky laugh and stepped back from him. Her hands trembled as she unlocked the door, and all the while, she could feel the heat of his body at her back, enveloping her like a cloak.

The moment they were inside, and the door closed, Loch was on her. He tangled his fingers through Mairi's hair and pulled her head back, while his lips traced her jawline and neck. His teeth nipped at the curve of her shoulder, and she shuddered with need.

She wanted him so much; it consumed her like a fever in her blood.

He could tear off her clothing right here in the common room and take her over one of the tables, and she'd welcome it. She didn't care if anyone walked in and saw them; she was too lost for that.

It was just as well that the inn was empty tonight.

Scooping her up into his arms, Loch turned and carried her up the stairs, his boots creaking on wood. Mairi entwined her arms about his neck and traced the length of his throat with her tongue and teeth, nipping gently as he'd done with her.

Loch stumbled but managed to reach the landing above without falling. He then carried her swiftly along the narrow hallway. Mairi had hung a lantern from the wall before going out earlier. It was guttering now, although it gave him just enough light to see by. "Is yer chamber the third on the right?" he rasped.

"Aye," she murmured as she tangled her fingers in his thick dark hair.

18: NO MORE PERFECT MOMENT THAN THIS

LOCH YANKED THE handle and shoved the door open with his shoulder.

An instant later, they were through. The door swung shut behind them, and Mairi found herself pressed up against it, Loch's mouth on hers.

He kissed her now without restraint, with a fevered hunger that unleashed her own.

The need between them was sharper than it had ever been in the past. She'd never been so desperate for him as she was now. As such, her body shook as he shoved her cloak from her shoulders and pushed down her sleek charcoal-colored gown.

"This dress," he growled. "Leaves *nothing* to the imagination." He shrugged off the fur mantle about his shoulders, letting it fall to the floor, before scooping her heavy breasts in his hands and lifting them high. Her swollen nipples were ruddy in the light of the glow of the nearby hearth. "Hades ... these are even more glorious than I remember."

With a deep sigh, he then lowered his head and feasted upon her breasts, suckling, lapping, and nipping until Mairi writhed against him. Her hands had fisted his hair now, slowly tightening as he continued to devour her.

Eventually, Loch pulled back and pushed her dress down farther, allowing it to pool around her ankles, leaving her naked before him. His gaze never left her as he heeled off his boots and began to unlace his tight leather trews.

Mairi's gaze lingered upon his broad chest, descending to where the crisp dark hair tapered to a vee down his stomach. And when he pushed down the breeches, his shaft sprang up, heavy and curved.

Mairi gave a soft cry at the sight of it—and then, without thinking about what she was doing, she sank to her knees before him.

Gaze fixed upon his straining rod, she cradled his bollocks with one hand while the other wrapped around his hard length. She then stroked him with slow, deliberate motions.

Loch gave a low curse, and Mairi bent her head, her hungry mouth fastening around him. His ragged groan filled the chamber.

A thrill feathered through Mairi at his response. She'd forgotten the feral sounds Loch made during their coupling, and how they'd once excited her.

She drew him deep, sighing at how good he tasted, and then she slid her mouth up and down his shaft, flicking her tongue under the crown of his swollen rod.

Loch's hands tangled in her hair, tightening as she worked him.

Arousal pulsed between Mairi's thighs. She'd also forgotten how much she'd enjoyed pleasuring him like this, the blend of submission and power in it.

Loch stopped her then, his breathing rough. He stepped back, hauling Mairi to her feet before throwing her onto the bed. Lying on her back, panting with need, she gazed up at him. Loch gripped her hips and yanked her forward so that her backside perched on the edge.

Mairi watched him spread her thighs wide, and then he sank to his knees on the floor between them.

He gazed at her sex, his eyes hooded, his lips parted. It was an intensely carnal look, one that made heat flush over her. She suddenly felt exposed, vulnerable. Nonetheless, she didn't cringe away; instead, she let him look all he wanted.

Without a word, Loch buried his face between her thighs and tasted her, with the same hunger as he had her breasts.

Within moments, Mairi was lost. She was vaguely aware of her throaty cries filling the chamber, of writhing and squirming under his wicked mouth, yet the aching pleasure that coiled in her loins, that made her thighs tremble and turned her body molten, quickly overwhelmed her.

And before she knew it, she shattered, hard, against his mouth.

Loch held her tightly as the storm passed, but when Mairi collapsed onto the mattress, he pushed himself off the floor and flipped her over onto her hands and knees.

The bed ropes creaked as he climbed onto the bed behind her.

Mairi was still gasping in the aftermath of what he'd just done, but Loch pushed her thighs wide, exposing her to him once more. She felt his hot gaze on her, feasting upon every exposed inch. Mairi whimpered and began to tremble in anticipation of what was to come.

Loch slid a finger deep into her, and she groaned.

"Ye are so wet, lass," he said throatily. "Are ye ready for me?"

"Aye," Mairi breathed.

She ached for him.

She felt the thick crown of his shaft then, pressing against her entrance, and pushed back against it, welcoming him.

With a groan, he sank into her in one long, deep slide.

Mairi cried out, pleasure trembling through her belly at the sensation of being filled. It had been so long, and he felt so good.

The ache of being stretched to the limit made her gasp. Memories, ones that had faded with the years, came crashing back—although this was even better than she remembered.

Her lover had returned to her; in that moment, everything seemed right with the world.

Loch plowed her in slow thrusts, as if savoring every moment. And all the while, he whispered wicked things that made heat flush over her, made her whimper, made her push back against him as she gasped needy pleas.

Loch leaned over Mairi then, his back sliding against hers. He braced himself against the bed with one hand, while the other slipped between her thighs, holding her up. The pad of his finger circled and teased as he continued to plow her.

Pleasure coiled and throbbed in Mairi's loins, and she started to tremble. Her eyes fluttered shut, and she ground against Loch, driving him deeper with each thrust.

With a guttural cry, she went over the edge again, only this time was even more intense than the first—and this time, wet heat pulsed deep within her womb.

Writhing against him, she was vaguely aware that he'd grabbed hold of her hips with both hands now and was plunging into her like a man possessed.

The wave of ecstasy within her peaked once more, and then, suddenly, Loch gave a ragged groan, his fingers digging into her hips.

He thrust home one last time and then bucked hard against her, letting himself go.

There was no more perfect moment than this.

Lying on his back with his lover's long, shapely limbs wrapped around him, her dark hair spread out like a curtain over his bare chest, Loch didn't let himself think for a while.

He soaked it in, let it cocoon him.

Mairi was asleep, her breath feathering against his skin. She'd rested her head in the hollow of his shoulder, as she had that day years earlier after he'd taken her amongst the heather.

The memory made something twist sharply in his chest before uneasiness filtered in.

What have I done?

Just like years earlier, there was always an 'afterward'. There were always repercussions. Responsibilities. And this time, he couldn't set sail for the mainland without a backward glance—nor did he want to.

Mairi's bedchamber was dark now, illuminated barely by the dying lump of peat in the hearth. Even so, Loch let his gaze roam over his surroundings. It was easier to focus on externals, even if he now felt as if he was intruding.

This room represented the woman in his arms. It was her private space, one that she'd furnished with brightly colored cushions and soft sheepskins. A patchwork hung from the lime-washed wall. Earlier, before the fire had died, he'd noted that it was made of squares of brown, green, and purple—the colors of the hills of Mull in the summer, when the heather was in bloom.

The tension in his chest twisted once more, and Loch closed his eyes.

In the aftermath of their encounter, he felt uncomfortably exposed. He never let himself go, yet when he'd been buried deep inside Mairi, he'd felt an overwhelming sense of homecoming. And afterward, as he'd cradled her close, wrapping his arms tightly about her, emotion swamped him. His throat had ached, and his eyelids had burned. Christ's blood, he'd been close to tears.

Fortunately, Mairi hadn't wanted to talk. Their coupling had exhausted them both, and she'd been serene afterward, content to be held, to enjoy his closeness. Loch was grateful that Mairi had fallen asleep. It gave him time to pull himself together.

Ever since his return to Mull, ever since being reunited with his leannan, he'd been drawn to Mairi again, unable to shake her from his thoughts. But now that she'd welcomed him into her arms, and her bed, once more, Loch wasn't sure what came next.

He'd never asked her if she'd been with anyone else in their years apart—yet instinctively, he knew she hadn't. She was a woman without guile. And she'd lain with Loch because her feelings for him hadn't waned.

But she would expect things from him now, things he couldn't give.

Heaving a deep breath, Loch shifted his gaze to the low beams overhead.

His gut hardened then, and he inwardly berated himself. *Idiot ... what did ye think would happen?*

19: BRIGHTER AND BETTER

"DO YE WANT more bannock?"

Loch shook his head, his mouth curving into a rueful smile. "I've just scoffed down a whole wheel ... I think I'd better stop now."

Mairi smiled back, brushing the crumbs off her skirts. They sat opposite each other before the hearth in her bedchamber, breaking their fast together with freshly-baked bannock, butter, and honey. She'd also brought up some weak ale from the kitchen, for they were both thirsty.

The meal had passed companionably, but now that the sky was lightening outdoors, Loch would soon be on his way.

Mairi's chest tightened. How she wished she could drag them both back in time, to relive the night before. It had passed all too quickly, and when she'd awoken in Loch's arms, and she'd spied the first glimmer of dawn peeking around the sacking covering the window, she'd wanted to chase the day away.

To greedily claim more time with her leannan.

Loch had already been awake and had pressed a tender kiss to her mouth in greeting. She'd hoped he'd tumble her again, for desire quickened low in her belly at the sight of him. Yet he'd slapped her lightly on the backside and informed her he was hungry.

Mairi's belly had growled in response, and so she'd donned clothing and gone downstairs to make them some bannock.

She'd expected to see Alison already in the kitchen, stoking the fire, but her cousin was nowhere to be seen. Deciding the lass was no doubt sleeping off too much mulled wine, Mairi placed a fresh lump of peat on the fire and quickly made another wheel of bannock.

And when she returned to her bedchamber, she'd found Loch dressed in his tight-fitting leather trews and boots, sitting by the fire.

The sight of him there, his dark hair mussed from sleep, his chest bare, had made her stomach flutter.

She couldn't believe that he was here, in her bedchamber. The man she'd never been able to cast from her heart had come back to her.

She wanted to prolong this moment, to enjoy the happiness that cocooned her.

Reaching out, Mairi gently traced the thin scar that slanted across his forehead with a fingertip. "How did ye get this?" she murmured.

"A slashing dagger-blade during a battle. He aimed for my eye … and missed."

Mairi winced. Loch spoke about such things with a nonchalant manner, as if nearly losing an eye were an everyday occurrence. She supposed it had been.

Silence fell between them then, and Mairi tensed. She wanted to talk to him longer yet sensed his rising impatience.

"I should be on my way, lass," Loch announced, rising to his feet.

Disappointment quickening within her, Mairi nodded. She too got up and went to fetch his cloak that she'd hung on the back of the door.

She passed it to him, and their fingers brushed. Loch's gaze hooded at the contact, and Mairi's breathing grew shallow. Desire shivered between them, turning the air heavy.

Her heart stuttered. How she wished for him to drag her back to bed and swive her until neither of them could move.

Loch stepped close then, his hand lifting to brush her cheek. "I shall see ye soon," he murmured.

"Aye," she whispered back, joy swelling in her chest. There was so much she wanted to say to him, yet she didn't know where to start. She didn't want to appear desperate, or to shatter the fragile thing that had blossomed between them. Likewise, Loch hadn't spoken of what the night before meant to him—or how it would change things between them.

However, his promise now reassured her.

He leaned in then, his lips brushing across hers. She wasn't sure whether he'd intended the kiss to be brief or not, but the moment their mouths met, Loch gave a groan low in his throat and hauled her into his arms.

A heartbeat later, they were kissing hungrily, tongues tangling, bodies pressed together hard.

Growling a curse, Loch tore his mouth from hers and trailed his lips down her jaw and throat. "God strike me down, Mairi," he groaned. "I can't get enough of ye."

Her breathing hitched, need pulsing through her. "Nor I of ye," she gasped.

His mouth covered hers once more, and they kissed again, desperately now.

And then, before Mairi knew what was happening, Loch had walked her back against the closed door. He lifted her skirts and spread her legs, as he yanked at the laces of his trews.

Panting, Mairi helped him release his swollen shaft before he pinned her hard against the door. He grasped Mairi's right knee then, lifting her leg high.

An instant later, he thrust into her, sheathing himself to the hilt.

Mairi cried his name, while Loch took her hard against the door, driving into her almost savagely. She ground against him with each thrust, desperate to bring him deeper.

The night before, he'd brought her to climax first, but this morning they went over the edge together. Mairi gasped and shuddered against Loch as he buried his face in her shoulder to muffle his deep groan.

They clung together, up against the door, for a while afterward, their breathing ragged.

Mairi stirred first, pushing the dark hair off his face. She then gently cupped his jaw and lifted his face so she could look at him.

Their gazes met, and her still-racing pulse kicked up into a gallop. He'd never looked at her like that, with such tenderness and vulnerability.

But there was something else in Loch's eyes this morning, something she couldn't quite fathom. He appeared, almost, sad.

Reaching up again, she stroked his bearded jaw. "That was a fine way to start the morning," she murmured. She wanted to chase away the shadows from his eyes.

Loch's mouth quirked. "I only intended to give ye a chaste kiss."

She gave a soft snort. There was nothing chaste about Loch Maclean. "Ye and I both know ye'd make a poor monk," she teased.

He laughed and moved back, withdrawing from her.

Mairi sighed, a sense of loss arrowing through her chest. She wanted him to stay. There was no better feeling than having him buried deep inside her. Couldn't they both cast aside their responsibilities, just for one day?

As if reading her thoughts, Loch lifted a hand, covering where hers still cupped his cheek. "Now, I really had better go," he said, regret lacing his voice. "Or someone will come looking for me."

Loch departed, slipping out of the inn into a bright, sharp morning, while Mairi busied herself in her morning routine. Firstly, she swept the floor of the common room and stocked the great hearth with fuel, humming to herself as she worked. Then, she made her way into the kitchen, where she started mixing some bread dough. As she kneaded it, a dreamy smile curved her lips.

Everything in the world seemed brighter and better today. Even making her usual batch of oaten bread, a task that she'd done every morning for years now, filled her with joy.

It wasn't a busy morning anyway, for there hadn't been any guests at the inn the eve before, and so there were no beds to make or bannocks to prepare for hungry merchants, farmers, and hunters who passed this way.

As she worked, Mairi's thoughts kept returning to Loch. They hadn't spoken of the future, or what would happen next. Nonetheless, he'd made it clear she'd see him soon.

She finished kneading the dough and placed a damp cloth over it, to allow it to rise. Going to the window, she opened the shutters, breathed in the crisp, salt-laced air, and gazed up at the clear morning sky. Her pulse quickened then. She couldn't wait to be in her lover's arms again—it was where she belonged.

Yet as she stood at the window, something uneasy stirred within her. It was like a tickle, a whisper, urging her to listen, yet she did her best to ignore it.

Nothing would intrude on her happiness today; she wouldn't let it.

While the bread dough was rising, Mairi started on a mutton stew. She was halfway through chopping onions and carrots for it, and singing a merry tune, when Alison appeared.

"I haven't heard ye sing that one in years," her cousin greeted her.

"Aye, well ... it's a lovely morning," Mairi replied. Straightening up, she cast an eye over Alison. Her cousin still wore her guise from the night before, although it appeared a little crumpled and grass-stained. Her blonde hair was slightly mussed as if she'd slept rough. "Mother Mary, where have ye been?"

Alison flashed her a sheepish smile but didn't elaborate.

"Are ye hungry?" Mairi gestured to the two wedges of bannock she and Loch had left earlier.

"Aye," Alison replied eagerly. She pulled up a stool at the table and helped herself to a bannock, spreading honey on it before taking a large bite.

Mairi flashed her an incredulous look as she resumed chopping carrots. "Didn't ye avail yerself of soul cakes yestereve?"

"Aye," Alison mumbled with her mouth full. "But after a night being tumbled by Tor under the stars … I've quite an appetite."

20: THE HOLLOW PROMISE

MAIRI ABRUPTLY STOPPED chopping, her gaze flying wide. "What?"

Alison's lips curved into a coy smile. "Ye heard me."

Mairi ran another, appraising, eye over her cousin. Of course, she should have recognized the serene expression on Alison's face, the slightly glazed look in her eyes. Mairi wagered *she* looked no different this morning—apart from the rumpled clothing and grass stains.

"I didn't realize the two of ye were ..." Mairi's voice trailed off. She'd never been comfortable talking about such things, even with her cousin.

"Attracted to each other?" Alison popped another piece of bannock into her mouth and chewed hungrily. After she'd swallowed, she favored Mairi with another smile. "Aye ... it's been brewing for a while now." Her expression turned soft then. "But it was last night that I realized I loved him." A blush rose to her cheeks as she added, "Tor is a shy lad ... and didn't know how to approach me. But I've helped him overcome his awkwardness."

Mairi inclined her head. "Hadn't he ever lain with a lass?" That surprised her. Most men of Tor's age had already tumbled a few women.

Alison cast her another coy look, making it clear that she wouldn't betray his confidence by revealing anything else.

Mairi finished chopping the carrots and tipped them and the onions she'd already diced into the cauldron. The vegetables hissed as they hit the hot pig fat she'd melted. Humming to herself, she then grabbed a long-handled wooden spoon and stirred.

Alison didn't have anything else to say on the matter, and when Mairi glanced her cousin's way once more, she saw that Alison was now studying *her*.

"There's something different about ye this morning," Alison murmured. "Ye aren't usually so chirpy."

Mairi shrugged, deliberately not elaborating. She then arched an eyebrow. "So ... what are Tor's intentions?"

Alison smiled once more—and this time, her smile wasn't secretive. Instead, it radiated pure joy. "He has asked me to become his wife ... and I have accepted."

Mairi gasped, dropping the wooden spoon. "He offered for ye?"

Alison beamed, her brown eyes gleaming now. "Aye."

"Oh, Ali ... that's wonderful." She went to her cousin then and pulled her into a fierce hug. She meant it too. Mairi hadn't spent much time with the young man who'd returned from the war with Loch. However, what she had seen of Tor Gordon indicated that he was a good-hearted lad. And after what Alison had suffered at that feckless fisherman's hands a year earlier, her cousin deserved a man she could trust with her heart.

Pulling back, she gazed down at Alison's face. The lass looked on the brink of tears—happy tears though.

"Will ye go to live at Duart?" she asked softly. Of course, she'd miss Alison, and it looked as if she'd be hiring not one, but two more locals to help her run the inn. Nonetheless, that didn't matter at present. She was keen to see Alison settled in a life of her choosing.

Alison met her eye, her mouth curving. "We'd like to live here, if ye'd allow it, Mairi?" she replied, her voice husky now.

"But I thought Tor was training to be a warrior?"

"Aye ... and he will aid the laird if he ever calls for him. But Tor also knows how much work the inn is for ye ... and he wishes to help."

Mairi stared at her. A moment later, her vision swam, and her throat thickened. "That's decent of him," she murmured, blinking as a tear escaped and trickled down her cheek. Indeed, she was overcome. "And of course, he is welcome."

"Thank ye, Mairi!" Alison threw her arms around Mairi's neck, hugging her tightly.

They clung together for a few moments in silence, the sound of sizzling vegetables reminding Mairi that she needed to tend her stew. However, she ignored it.

Despite her happiness for her cousin, a little of the joy that had cocooned Mairi this morning fell away. Suddenly, the day wasn't quite as bright. It was as if a shadow had passed over the sun.

All she could think about was that she and Alison had both spent the night with men they loved, but they'd ended quite differently.

Tor had proposed to Alison and would make her his wife—while Loch had walked away with nothing more than a promise to see her again.

The contrast made uneasiness stir within her once more.

The days passed, two sliding into three, and three into four—but Loch didn't return to *The Craignure Inn*.

Mairi looked out for him, of course. Every time the door to the inn opened, her gaze cut to it, hope rising in her breast. Especially in the evenings, when he was most likely to show his face, she found herself constantly watching the door.

But the days continued to pass, and there was no sign of her leannan.

Mairi did her best not to worry.

It helped that running the inn kept her busy. She shopped for food, took deliveries, and ordered more ale from the local brewer. Work on the new wing was progressing well. Muir's team had finished building the walls, and a carpenter was now putting up the framing for the roof. Mairi had just contacted the local thatcher, who'd begin work as soon as they were done.

And all the while, Mairi tried to keep a positive outlook, to tell herself Loch hadn't forgotten her.

However, by the seventh day, her belly was in knots. Her appetite had dulled, and her patience shortened. A full week had passed since they'd lain together, since he'd promised they'd see each other soon. And still no sign of him.

It grew steadily more difficult to reassure herself that nothing was wrong. And increasingly, despair crept in.

On the eve of the seventh day, Mairi found it hard to concentrate, despite that the inn was even busier than usual. It was even harder to smile, to pretend her heart wasn't slowly breaking.

Counting her takings at the end of the night, after the last of the customers had departed, she found herself blinking rapidly as her vision blurred with tears. *He made ye a hollow promise, lass,* she told herself. *Ye were a fool to take him at his word.*

"Mairi … is something amiss?"

Mairi glanced up to find Alison watching her. Her cousin sat opposite her at the high bench, washing tankards in a pail of hot, soapy water.

Concern shadowed Alison's gaze.

Mairi shook her head, even as her throat started to ache. Lord, she wished she could keep her hurt inside, yet it clawed at her now, demanding release.

Alison put down the tankard she'd just washed and leaned forward, placing a damp hand on Mairi's arm. "Something has happened between ye and the laird … hasn't it?"

Mairi swallowed. She'd avoided this subject all week. All the same, she'd seen Alison observing her during the past days. Aye, she'd noted the gradual change in her mood, her ratcheting tension before sadness and resignation set in.

"I feel like a fool," she admitted then, placing the last stack of silver pennies they'd taken in that eve into the safe box. "At eight and twenty, I should have known better."

Alison's gaze widened. "Ye have lain with him, haven't ye?"

Mairi nodded. God's teeth, the shame of it. She suddenly felt as if their roles had been reversed. For years, she'd been Alison's caretaker, as protective of her as an older sister would have been. She'd always prided herself on being the sensible one—yet when it came to men, Alison was clearly the wiser of the two of them.

After suffering for love, her cousin had learned to choose more wisely, and she'd given her heart to someone truly worthy. Tor wouldn't toy with Alison's heart the way Loch had done with hers. No, he'd cherish her.

The young warrior had visited the inn every evening since Samhuinn. And to Mairi's surprise, he hadn't spent his time chatting to Alison and distracting her from her work. Instead, he'd helped out for an hour or two, serving ale and dealing with any rowdy patrons.

Earlier that eve, he'd broken up a fight between two customers.

Tor had returned to Duart Castle now, as he did every night. He and Alison had planned their wedding for the first day of December—three weeks hence—and Alison was making a dress for the occasion. Every eve, after they finished in the inn, the two cousins worked on it for a while.

"Don't blame yerself for this," Alison murmured, squeezing her arm. Her mouth tugged into a smile then. "I imagine Loch Maclean is difficult to resist."

"Aye, he is," Mairi admitted huskily. "I know he's the clan-chief and I'm an innkeeper's daughter ... but I've always believed that our different ranks didn't really matter ... that love would somehow find a way." A tear escaped then, rolling down her cheek, although she quickly dashed it away. "But Loch wants nothing more than an occasional tumble ... while I want" —Mairi broke off there, her throat so tight it was difficult to talk— "his heart."

Her cousin's pretty features tightened. "Ye love him still, don't ye?"

"Aye." The admission made Mairi's stomach hurt. "I never stopped loving him." Squeezing her eyes shut, she swallowed convulsively. Lord, this hurt. It now felt as if fists were pummeling her insides. "And that's why he has the power to destroy me."

21: WILLFULLY BLIND

"A MISSIVE HAS come ... from my brother," Jack announced as he strode, without knocking, into the solar.

Loch glanced up from where he'd been spooning honey on his porridge and took the roll of parchment. Sure enough, the wax seal had the imprint of a thistle upon it—belonging to the Macleans of Dounarwyse.

"Take a seat," he said, nodding to the table. "I'd prefer to read this without ye looming over me."

Making an impatient sound in the back of his throat, Jack pulled back a chair and flung himself ungraciously into it. He then cast a gaze to where Astrid sat, pale and silent, at the opposite end of the table to her brother. "Morning, Lady Astrid."

She nodded to him yet said nothing.

Loch cast his sister a weary look. The two of them always broke their fast together in his solar. However, ever since he'd promised her to Kendric Mackinnon, Astrid said little to him at mealtimes.

The lass was picking at the wedge of bannock before her, which wasn't anything new. Of late, she'd lost her appetite. She was already slender, but the flesh had started to melt off her bones.

Loch's brow furrowed as he observed her. Astrid looked frail this morning. He didn't like seeing her so thin.

Still frowning, he shifted his attention to the missive and broke the seal before unfurling it. He then began to read.

"Well?" Jack probed, not bothering to curb his impatience. "What does Rae have to say?"

"He confirms that the Mackinnons have given back the lands we asked for," Loch replied. "He has moved his cottars from Faing Burn, north of Dounarwyse Castle."

Jack murmured an oath, under his breath, his green eyes glinting. "I don't believe it … the shitweasel kept his word. I never thought I'd see the day."

"I too had my doubts," Loch admitted. "But it seems he wants my sister." He glanced up, his attention traveling once more to Astrid.

She met his gaze, her eyes glittering. "I suppose this will make ye quite the hero," she said, her tone sharp. Her hand was clenched around her eating knife, her knuckles white. "The wild lad who went away to war … but then came back and redeemed himself. Next time ye go into Craignure, mothers will ask ye to kiss their bairns."

Loch's mouth pursed. He'd suffered from the odd pang of guilt over the past weeks, at seeing how upset his sister was at the alliance he'd made, yet her blade-like tongue now hardened his heart. "Ye need to ready yerself, Astrid," he said coolly. "Mackinnon will call for ye soon."

Finn strode into the solar then, his light-brown hair mussed. He'd clearly been outside already, overseeing the guards, as strong gusts battered the walls of the keep this morning.

"God's troth," Loch muttered. "Don't either of ye know how to knock?"

"A head of cattle has gone missing on the shores of Loch Ba," Finn announced, ignoring his complaint.

Loch scowled. "How in Hades do ye know that?"

"A farmer has just arrived. The man's incensed … and he's in the outer courtyard now, if ye wish to speak to him?"

Loch grunted, threw down his porridge spoon, and rose to his feet.

These days, he couldn't even break his fast in peace. The past week had flown, with one problem after the other to deal with. The bailiff had hauled in three farmers who refused to pay their rents, and then he'd had to settle a dispute between two families in Duart village after a farmer cuckolded his neighbor.

Frankly, he was sick of it—and the news of the stolen cattle put him in a sour mood.

However, he hadn't even moved away from the table when his sister spoke once more. "It'll be the Mackinnons."

Loch cut Astrid a sharp look. "Ye don't know that, lass."

Astrid stood up, bristling with indignance. "Loch Ba is but a stone's throw from our border with the Mackinnons," she pointed out. "Of course, it's them."

"She has a point, Loch," Jack muttered, his auburn brows drawing together.

Loch's lips thinned as he looked to Finn. "Did the farmer see who took them?"

Finn shook his head.

"Aye … well then, *none* of us have any proof." Loch fixed his sister with a hard stare. "And until we do, I'll not assume the Mackinnons are behind this."

"The proof is before ye," Astrid ground out. "But ye are willfully blind."

"It is ye who is blinkered," he replied. "By yer reluctance to wed the Mackinnon clan-chief."

"Reluctance?" Her tone turned shrill. "Cloth-eared dolt! If ye give me to him, my life will be *over!*"

Finn muttered something under his breath then, about shrewish women who could do with a scold's bridle.

And an instant later, Astrid grabbed her eating knife from the table and hurled it at Finn. The blade spun through the air and thudded into the wooden shield mounted on the wall behind him, narrowly missing his head.

Silence fell in the solar, and then Luag, who'd been sitting next to the hearth, gave a low growl.

Finn's face went taut. He turned and yanked the knife out of the shield. "Satan's cods," he growled. "Ye could have killed me, woman."

"It's a pity my aim was off," Astrid spat. "Or ye'd be choking yer last breath right now." Her mouth twisted then. "And ye'd deserve it too, for *murdering* my friend!"

The rasp of Finn's sharp inhale followed. His hazel eyes narrowed into slits, a nerve ticking in his cheek. His lips parted then as he readied himself to answer, but he didn't get the chance.

"Astrid!" Loch's voice lashed across the solar, his patience finally snapping. "Ye go too far." He crossed to her then, took hold of her arm, and steered her toward the door. "Out!"

"Where are ye taking me?" she snarled, struggling. "To the dungeons, so I can sit amongst the rats?"

Loch was sorely tempted. Perhaps a spell in that fetid hole would improve her attitude. "No," he bit out. "To yer bedchamber ... where ye can wait out the rest of the day."

Loch was still quietly simmering when he descended the steps to the ground floor of the keep, Luag padding silently behind him. The cattle farmer was waiting for him in the outer courtyard, but first, he'd had to escort his sister to her room.

In truth, he was at his wits end over how to handle Astrid. The sooner Mackinnon wed her the better.

What a week it had been. He'd had hardly a moment to himself. On days like this, he wished for nothing more than to saddle a fast horse and gallop away, leaving his troubles behind him. He had a new respect for his father now. Surely, it was the heavy weight of responsibility that had sent him to an early grave.

However, as he reached the bottom of the stairs and headed through the entrance hall to the large oaken door that would take him outside, Loch's pulse quickened.

Mairi.

He'd told her he'd see her soon, yet he'd let seven full days pass. He could have sent word with Tor, for the lad visited *The Craignure Inn* every evening these days. Tor was smitten with Mairi's bonnie cousin and had even proposed to her. They'd marry within a few weeks, and Mairi had agreed to allow Tor to help run the inn.

Discovering that Mairi would have a man working at the inn, to assist where necessary, had pleased Loch. And yet it also left him feeling unsettled.

Mairi would be worrying now, wondering why he'd stayed away.

Even though he was busy, he could have spared her some time. But he hadn't.

It wasn't as if Loch hadn't thought about her. In fact, he had—constantly. And that was the problem. Mairi had gotten under his skin; she made him feel exposed. Weak.

Outdoors, an icy wind howled across the inner courtyard, sending dust devils scattering. Loch had tied his hair back at his nape, although strands of it whipped free immediately, stinging his eyes. Even Luag lowered his head, to brace himself against the wind. It blew the dog's wiry hair back from its face as it loped next to Loch.

These days, the wolfhound was determined to be his shadow—and, in truth, there was something comforting about Luag's company.

Loch strode toward the archway that would take him through to the outer courtyard, and with effort, pushed Mairi from his thoughts.

I'll visit her soon, he reassured himself, *but for the moment, there's work to be done.*

A storm battered the walls of Duart Castle that evening; icy needles of rain and hail lashed in from the north.

It was a night to be indoors, cozied up by a roaring fire. But even so, once supper had ended and Loch retired, alone, to his solar with a cup of wine, he couldn't settle.

A brooding mood had descended upon him, coupled with an impatience that made him tap his foot as he sat before the hearth.

Likewise, Luag didn't relax either. Usually, the wolfhound stretched out before the fire and ended up snoring so loudly that Loch had to nudge the beast with his foot.

Not this eve. Instead, Luag approached Loch, head down, and pressed against his leg.

"What do ye want, lad?" Loch muttered, even as he reached down and stroked the wolfhound's ears.

Luag's long tail started to wag, although he gave a whine.

"Aye, I'm not myself tonight either," Loch said, his gaze shifting to the dancing flames in the hearth.

The dog sat back on its haunches and watched him with soulful brown eyes.

Loch sighed. "I should go to her, shouldn't I?"

Luag's tail started thumping on the sheepskin before the hearth.

"Right." Loch pushed himself out of his chair. "Fancy a night ride in the wind and rain?"

Luag fell in behind him, giving Loch his answer. The dog's claws clicked on the wooden floor as he followed his master toward the solar door. However, Loch was just a yard from the door when it opened and Finn strode in, nearly colliding with him.

His friend's shoulder-length hair was plastered back against his scalp, and he wore a dripping sealskin cloak about his shoulders. The grim look on Finn's face immediately warned Loch that something was wrong.

"What is it?" he demanded.

"It's yer sister," Finn replied, biting out the words as if merely speaking about Astrid galled him. "She's missing."

22: HUNTING ASTRID

"HOW THE DEVIL did she get out of the castle without anyone seeing?" Loch snarled as he took the steps, two at a time, descending to the bottom level of the keep.

"Someone *did*," Finn replied from behind him. "Astrid talked the guard at the gate into letting her out just after dusk ... said she had to go urgently to Craignure." Scorn crept into Finn's voice then as he continued. "The lad was besotted with her ... apparently, she promised him *favors* upon her return."

Loch growled a curse. He'd deal with the lust-addled fool later. Right now, his focus was on finding his sister. "Christ's blood," he muttered. "Where does she think she's going in this weather?"

Finn didn't answer.

They left the refuge of the keep behind and stepped into the howling night, hastening to the outer courtyard, to where Jack and Tor had just readied their horses in the stables. For once, Tor hadn't gone to *The Craignure Inn*. The vile weather had kept him inside the castle tonight.

Tor's face was taut with worry as he handed Loch the reins to his horse. "Do we know which way she went?"

"The guard says Craignure ... but he didn't actually *see* her head north," Jack replied.

"She'll be looking to get off the isle," Loch answered tersely. For some reason, it was clear to him what his sister would do. "But Craignure is too close ... and there won't be a ferry until late morning ... that's if the weather clears. I'd wager she'll travel to another port and try to find passage there."

"Donian would be the obvious choice," Finn said. "She'd likely reach it overnight … and be ready to leave with the dawn."

"Aye … that's where I'd head if I were Astrid," Loch agreed. "Come. Enough talk. We need to catch up with her."

Mounted on fast coursers, wrapped up in sealskins and fur, and carrying guttering pitch torches, the four warriors clattered out of the outer courtyard, under the portcullis, and down the causeway into the village. Luag ran at Loch's side, a fleet shadow in the darkness.

Outside the protective walls of the fortress, the night was even fouler than they'd anticipated. The wind pulled at Loch's clothing like rough hands and stung his exposed cheeks. Bent low over the saddle, he squinted ahead at the small circle of light his torch revealed.

And all the while, anger beat like a battle drum in his chest.

When he found his sister, he was going to throttle her.

They rode through the night, reaching Donian with the first glimmers of dawn.

The storm spent itself in the early hours, leaving a misty veil over the isle, and when the first rays of light peeked through from the east, they revealed a bleak, windswept landscape.

Donian perched on the edge of a white-sand beach, framed by a sparse growth of twisted, wind-blasted oaks. It was a fishing village where hardy fishermen struck out onto the waters of the sound daily, bringing back catches of mackerel, pollock, and coalfish, much of which they sold across the water at the busy port of Oban.

Now that the weather was clearing, Loch caught sight of fishermen on the beach. Some of them were calling out to each other as they readied their nets, while others were already pushing their boats out into the water. The Sound of Mull was as smooth as a polished garnet this morning, in the wake of the storm.

Loch urged his courser on, racing ahead of his companions as he approached the shore. Luag sped next to him, tongue lolling.

Astrid would be down there somewhere, Loch knew it.

And as his horse galloped out onto the beach, spraying sand up from under its hooves, he spied a knot of men. Rough laughter echoed across the shore, followed by lewd shouts—and then Loch glimpsed a flash of pale hair in the midst of the group.

His heart lurched.

Astrid.

He'd expected to see her negotiating with one of the fishermen, or even perched in one of the boats being pushed out into the water.

Not surrounded, and in trouble.

Astrid's hair had come loose from its braid and tumbled in damp, messy curls around her face. However, she didn't look afraid—just enraged.

None of them had noticed the four men on horseback racing toward them, for their attention was fixed upon their prize. And as he neared, Loch realized that this mob weren't fishermen. There were no nets in the large rowboat beside them. They were dressed in dirty braies and tattered gambesons and had the look of smugglers.

Their voices rang out across the beach, carrying in the still morning air.

"A bonnie wee thing ye are," one of the men crooned.

"Aye," a companion agreed with a leer. "But I'd wager she'll look even prettier riding my rod."

This comment drew an explosion of rough laughter from his companions.

"Not before she's tasted mine," the first man replied. He then made a grab for Astrid, although his friends' amusement abruptly cut off when he gave a shout of pain. "The bitch cut me!"

Indeed, Astrid had drawn a blade and slashed him across the forearm with it. She now lowered to a crouch, her eyes glinting. "I'll geld the next one of ye to touch me," she warned.

Loch pulled up his courser and leaped off its back, drawing the dirk at his hip. "Aye, although that's kinder than what I'll do if any of ye lay a finger on my sister," he shouted.

Next to him, Luag's hackles rose, a feral growl rumbling from his throat.

The smugglers leaped back from Astrid, reaching for their weapons.

Meanwhile, Loch's companions had caught up and dismounted from their horses, flanking him.

Loch thought that would be enough to scatter the ragged band. But to his surprise, they held fast. One of them, the one who was nursing a cut across his forearm, snarled a curse and spat on the ground.

An instant later, he lunged for Loch.

The fight was short, but bloody. The smugglers were vicious, yet Loch, Jack, and Finn waded in as if they were going into battle. They fought shoulder-to-shoulder, their dirk-blades glinting in the dawn. Tor too was no stranger to violence, having just come from conflict, and Luag also leaped into the fray, teeth bared. Moments later, his jaws snapped tight around one of the smugglers' legs.

Anger continued to pound through Loch's veins as he gutted his first opponent. The man tried to stab him in the eye, yet Loch ducked and dove forward, slamming his dirk deep into the smuggler's belly.

Cries and grunts rose up from the beach, blending with the squawking of gulls and Luag's snarls.

And when it was done, only two of the six smugglers remained alive. The men whimpered as they lay, cradling bloodied limbs on the sand, while a crowd of fishermen had gathered nearby to watch the fight play out.

Astrid stood a few feet away as well, her knife still clutched in her right hand. Loch was surprised to see her still there. He thought she might attempt to run—however, it seemed her feet had grown roots. Perhaps she realized it was futile to try and escape him.

Ignoring his sister for the moment, Loch moved close to the two injured smugglers, his gaze roving over them.

"Where are ye from?" he asked coldly.

"Croig," one of the men wheezed.

Loch frowned. Croig was a small village on the northern coast of their isle—far from Maclean lands. "Ye are Mackinnons?"

"Aye."

Loch hunkered down, meeting the eye of the injured man. "I'm going to spare yer life," he said, his voice lowering. "But when ye return to the north and folk ask ye what happened, ye are to tell them that ye made the mistake of tangling with Loch Maclean."

The smuggler's hazel eyes widened.

Loch favored him with a thin smile. "Aye, that's right. And if I ever see yer face again, ye're a dead man."

Leaving the two injured smugglers where they lay, Loch gestured to Astrid, indicating that she was to mount his horse. He wasn't sure what she'd done with her own—most likely sold it to buy herself passage—although at present, he was too incensed to care.

His pulse still beat in his ears, but he managed to choke down his rage. He didn't want to talk to Astrid when he was this angry. He needed to calm down first.

He'd imagined his sister would snarl at him, yet perhaps sensing his simmering rage, she went meekly. All the same, her face was pale and drawn as she sheathed her dirk and then vaulted lightly up onto his horse.

Wordlessly, Loch mounted behind her, while Jack, Finn, and Tor recovered their coursers and did the same.

They rode home in silence, across bare hills, while the morning sky arched pale-blue above them. It was a rare windless day, although the air held a bite to it.

Loch barely noticed though.

Astrid perched in front of him, her slender body rigid as she anticipated the coming storm.

However, by the time the high walls of Duart Castle appeared to the northeast, Loch's temper had cooled a little. It was noon, and the aroma of stewing venison drifted through the outer courtyard as they dismounted their horses.

Father Hector came out to meet them, his angular face drawn with worry. "All is well?" he asked, as his gaze slid over brother and sister.

"No," Loch replied gruffly, throwing the reins to a stable lad. "Although things could be far worse." Aye, his sister had some skill with a dirk, but that wouldn't have saved her. She'd been outnumbered, six to one. Loch didn't want to think what would have happened to Astrid if he and his companions hadn't reached her in time.

His gut clenched then, his anger quickening once more. "Where's the guard who let her out?"

"They've put him in the dungeons," the chaplain replied. "Will ye hang him?"

Loch didn't reply, although Astrid made a soft choking sound at this news—her first real response since they'd taken her from Donian.

Loch turned to her. "Don't tell me ye care what happens to the man ye used in order to escape?" he growled.

Astrid raised her chin in a stubborn tilt. "Boyd is my friend."

"The lad is clearly besotted with ye," Loch shot back, his lip curling. "And ye know it too ... which is why ye made him a false promise."

"Don't kill him, Loch," Astrid gasped.

"Why not? Why shouldn't I make an example out of him?"

His sister's brown eyes glistened with tears and her throat worked convulsively. Suddenly, all the rebelliousness went out of her. "Don't!" She moved to him, her hands clutching at the sleeve of his gambeson. "Boyd isn't to blame for this ... ye are right. I knew he was soft on me ... and I made him ... promises."

"That doesn't excuse what he did," Loch replied. "My guards answer to *me*, not my sister."

"Spare him." Astrid's fingers dug into his arm. "Please!"

Loch's gaze fused with hers. "I tire of ye defying me Astrid," he muttered, "and after what ye have just put me through, ye are on shaky ground."

"I know," she gasped, tears running down her face now. "But I only did it because I was desperate ... because ye won't listen to me."

The anguish in her voice was an arrow through the chest, yet he hardened himself to it. He wouldn't let her manipulate him. "Astrid," he growled. "Don't ye start—"

"Very well!" she cried. "Ye win! I shall marry Mackinnon willingly. I ask only one thing of ye." She broke off then, her chest heaving from the force of the emotions roiling inside her. "Cast Boyd out, if ye must ... but don't hurt him for something that was *my* fault."

23: OLD HABITS

HE ARRIVED LATE, just as Mairi was about to bar the door for the night.

Loch ducked under the low lintel and entered the common room, his gaze sweeping over the warm space before it came to rest where she stood a few feet back from the hearth.

Mairi's breath rushed out of her, even as she cursed herself for responding to him so keenly. This man made her weak, needy—how she hated feeling this way.

And curse him too, for looking so virile, so perilously masculine. His thick dark hair was pulled back at the nape, and he wore a heavy fur mantle about his shoulders. His cheeks were slightly flushed with cold, for a frost was settling outdoors.

Mairi's heart started to thump like an angry fist.

God's teeth, why couldn't he have turned up days ago? Why had he given her time for every fear, every regret, to surface and gnaw at her? She'd been floating after their night together at Samhuinn, full of hope that this marked a new start for them.

But the long days that followed had told her the truth.

There was no new start—only old habits.

And now, here he was walking toward her as if nothing had changed.

Mairi tore her gaze from him and glanced over at her cousin. Alison had just emerged from the kitchen, a pail of hot water in hand.

"Leave that on the bench, Ali," she ordered softly. "I'll finish up down here."

Alison paused, her face tensing. However, unlike weeks earlier, when Loch had walked back into her life, her cousin didn't argue. Instead, she nodded and set the bucket down on the bench without a word. She then made for the stairs, casting a narrow-eyed look at Loch as she went.

The creak of the stairs followed as Alison went up to her bedchamber. When they were alone, Loch finally broke the heavy silence that had settled in the common room.

"Yer cousin doesn't look pleased with me."

"Doesn't she?" Mairi replied. Folding her arms across her chest, she raised her chin to glare at him. "I can't imagine why."

"Ye aren't pleased with me either," he noted.

Mairi clenched her jaw, willing him to turn around and leave. That was what he was good at anyway. "Why are ye here?"

"To see *ye*," Loch replied, moving closer. "I'm sorry I've stayed away so long."

Even with a few feet separating them, she felt his nearness—that cool, fresh scent that was uniquely his, blended with leather and woodsmoke.

That smell made longing twist under her ribs. But she pushed her need for this man aside. Her longing for Loch addled her mind and caused her to make bad choices.

She had to stay calm and rational. She had to remind herself of the decision she'd come to the night before as she'd lain abed, tears trickling down her cheeks.

This couldn't go on any longer.

"Ye have much to occupy ye, I'm sure," Mairi said, her voice flat.

"Ye don't know the half of it," he replied, pulling a face. "Since Samhuinn, I've had one problem after another to deal with ... and then Astrid ran off three days ago."

Mairi's brow furrowed. Tor had brought word of the incident. The news had upset Mairi, for she could only imagine how desperate Astrid must have been to have done such a thing. "And how is Lady Astrid faring?"

"Well enough," Loch replied brusquely, although his disgruntled expression warned that his sister was a sore subject with him at present. "Astrid rebelled against wedding the Mackinnon, but she has finally acquiesced ... and not before time."

Anger quickened in Mairi's belly. She'd told herself that when she saw Loch again, she'd keep a leash on her temper—that she'd deal with him calmly—but her resolution was proving harder than she thought.

Right now, she wished to slap him hard across the face. On his sister's behalf *and* her own.

"That's all women are to ye, aren't they," she said, her voice roughening. "We're pieces to be moved around an Ard-ri board. We're useful sometimes, aye ... if ye want to make a truce or earn yerself more land ... or if ye want sons to carry on yer bloodline." Mairi took a step toward him, placing her hands on her hips now. Loch's gaze had narrowed, yet she was just getting started. "And of course, we're good for humping whenever yer balls get too tight. Is that why ye are here, Loch? Are yer bollocks giving ye trouble?"

His bearded jaw tightened.

"I thought so," Mairi said, even as her heart started to pound once more. "Well, ye have made a wasted trip ... for I'll not be spreading my legs for ye."

Loch scowled. "Ye are not usually so crude, Mairi."

"No, I'm usually a fool."

A brittle silence fell, stretching out before Loch heaved a sigh. "I did want to visit earlier, lass," he began, his tone soothing as if he were gentling a skittish horse. "But—"

"Nine days, Loch." Mairi ground out. "Ye waited *nine* days before deigning to stop by. Some men would cross burning lands and wild seas for a woman ... but ye couldn't even make the half-hour ride between Duart and Craignure. That's how little I mean to ye."

Loch went still, his face tightening.

Mairi's belly twisted. He likely thought her hysterical, yet she didn't care. She was past caring. "It's over between us, Loch," she gasped, breathless with the hurt and anger that pummeled her. "But then, it never really began, did it?"

"Mairi." His voice was rough now. "Ye are taking this too hard. I was only—"

"No," she cut him off, shaking her head. "I don't want to hear it. I'm worth more than the crumbs ye throw me ... I always was." She gestured toward the door. "Please leave."

Their gazes met, and it was hard not to drown in the depths of those rich night-brown eyes. Once, she would have—but not any longer.

She braced herself for Loch to try again, for the excuses that slipped so easily off his tongue. She'd hardened her heart against them though. His absence had given her ample time to ready herself. And as the days had passed, she'd watched Tor turn up in all weathers to see Alison. The only eve he hadn't come was the night of the storm, the night Lady Astrid had run off.

Noting the tender smiles between Tor and Alison, the way he looked out for her, had been a knife to Mairi's heart. But it was necessary. She had to face the truth squarely for once.

Loch had never treated her like that, and he likely never would.

And Mairi wanted to be loved, to be treasured, as her father had once treasured her mother. To Loch, she would always be an afterthought.

Aye, she expected him to try and make more excuses for himself, yet he didn't.

Of course, Loch Maclean was too proud for that. Giving a curt nod, his expression shuttered now, he stepped back from her. He turned then and, without another word, made for the door. Opening it, he stepped out into the night, letting in a cold blast of air that made the flames in the hearth gutter.

And then he was gone, taking the tattered shreds of Mairi's girlish dreams, and her heart, with him.

"Is Astrid unwell?"

Loch glanced up from where he was inspecting a stone bruise on his stallion's hoof, to find his cousin leaning against a pillar inside the stables, arms folded across his chest. "No," he replied curtly before shifting his attention back to Falcon's hoof.

The horse must have trodden on something sharp during the ride back from Craignure the night before. It was hardly surprising, for Loch had ridden the courser fast through the icy night under the hoary light of the moon, heedless of the perilous cliffs just a few feet from the road. And as they'd clattered into the outer courtyard, he'd noticed the stallion was lame. Self-recrimination had spiked through Loch at the realization, drawing him from the black mood that had consumed him upon leaving the inn. He should have taken more care. Falcon was big-hearted and deserved better treatment.

After breaking his fast this morning, Loch had gone down to the stables to check on his horse—and that was where Jack had found him.

Moments passed, and when Jack said nothing else, Loch looked up once more to find his cousin studying him. "What?" he barked.

Jack arched an eyebrow. "I just met the lass on the stairs. She's as thin as a reed these days, and worryingly pale."

Loch sighed, lowering Falcon's hoof to the ground. He then straightened up and patted the stallion's flank. "She's been this way ever since I arranged her marriage to Mackinnon."

"Not like this," Jack said, shaking his head. "I think she's sickening."

Loch's gut tightened, even as he frowned. He stepped away from Falcon and ducked out of the stall. "It could be a ruse," he muttered. "She's told me she'll marry the

Mackinnon willingly … but since he confirmed the date for the second day of February … she's likely trying to come up with another way to get out of it."

Jack snorted. "Christ's blood, cousin … ye are harsh with yer sister."

Loch's frown slipped into a scowl. "And ye are too soft-hearted," he muttered.

"Astrid's a good lass," Jack replied with a shrug. "I don't like seeing her suffer."

"I don't either," Loch snapped. "This didn't have to be so hard … it's Astrid who's made it so."

The two men emerged from the stables into the outer courtyard. It was a still morning with a cloudless sky overhead. However, the air was so cold that their breathing steamed before them. They were heading toward winter now, and Yule. The nights had drawn in, and the last of the color upon the hills had faded.

Loch spied a slight figure then, crossing the courtyard. Astrid was heading toward the chapel, her head bowed. She hadn't seen him or Jack yet.

Observing her, Loch's mouth thinned. Maybe his cousin had a point. His sister didn't look herself at all these days. Her kirtle hung off her, and Astrid's once lustrous and vibrant pale-gold hair hung limply down her back. She wore a listless expression, and her step was heavy.

But the most worrying thing was her eyes. They were flat, resigned. It was as if the spark inside her had gone out.

Loch halted and watched as his sister disappeared into the chapel. Then, feeling his cousin's gaze upon him, he glanced over at Jack. "What is it now?" he demanded, his temper fraying.

Jack favored him with a rueful smile. "Ye have a furrow etched upon yer brow this morning," his cousin drawled. "Who pissed in yer porridge?"

The knots in Loch's stomach yanked tighter, bitterness filling his mouth as he recalled the insults Mairi had flung at him the night before. The worst thing was, she wasn't wrong about him—and her insight was galling. "*I* did," he muttered, turning away.

24: NO MENDING A BROKEN HEART

ALISON COULDN'T STOP smiling.

Standing before the doorway to Duart Castle's chapel—dressed in a lovely lavender kirtle, with a cream-colored shawl about her shoulders—Mairi's cousin radiated joy.

And despite that her soul ached these days, Mairi was happy for her.

Father Hector was now winding a length of red and green Maclean plaid around Tor and Alison's joined hands.

A chill wind gusted across the outer courtyard then, and Mairi shivered, drawing her heavy wool cloak close. It had been a long while since she'd stood inside Duart Castle, and she'd been reluctant to return today. However, Tor had asked the castle chaplain to wed them, and so she'd swallowed her hesitation and put on a brave face.

Loch was present, and she'd steeled herself to see him again. She wouldn't cast a shadow over Alison and Tor's happy day.

Mairi couldn't believe the wedding had crept up on them so quickly. November had slid by, and it was now the first day of December. It wasn't the best weather for such a celebration, although Alison and Tor couldn't have cared less. The crowd of well-wishers all huddled, like Mairi, under thick mantles, and Father Hector's shoulders were hunched with cold, although the bride and groom barely noticed the stinging wind.

The chaplain began the service then, his gravelly voice carrying across the courtyard.

Mairi kept her eyes forward, but after a short while, her skin prickled.

Someone was watching her, and she knew who it would be. She'd spied Loch the moment she walked into the courtyard under the portcullis. He was standing to the left of the chapel steps, Lady Astrid at his side.

As soon as Mairi had taken her place amongst the crowd, Loch's gaze snapped her way. In response, she'd hurriedly averted her own. And even as she felt the laird staring at her now, willing her to meet his eye, Mairi continued to ignore him. It was better that way.

Even so, shutting Loch out wasn't easy. Her traitorous soul still longed for him. Every day, she reminded herself of all the reasons why she'd done the right thing in severing contact with the man.

And as she began to sweat now, despite the cold, under the heat of his gaze, she kept repeating them to herself until the longing subsided.

He's arrogant and callous.

He's incapable of love.

He treated me like his plaything.

He broke my heart.

Loch clenched his jaw, frustration gathering like a storm inside him.

He hated being ignored.

Mairi had seen him, but she was intent on pretending he didn't exist. She stood amongst the well-wishers, a deep wine-red cloak wrapped tightly around her to ward off the cold. She looked comely indeed today, her dark hair whipping around her proud face, her tawny eyes luminous as she watched the ceremony.

Loch fisted his hands at his sides. Curse him to Hades, he missed her.

He'd stayed away from *The Craignure Inn* of late, had given Mairi's temper time to settle. However, from her reaction now, it was clear she was resolved.

Mairi wasn't playing games. She really did want nothing more to do with him.

Loch's breathing grew shallow. Of course, what Mairi truly desired was his heart, his soul, but the thought of giving himself over to her made him feel queasy. He wasn't truly vulnerable with *anyone*—and that was the way he liked it. Yet somehow, Mairi had gotten under his skin. Now, he wasn't sure how she'd managed such a feat or what to do about that.

Cheering erupted then, drawing Loch's attention.

The ceremony had concluded, and Tor drew Alison into his arms for a lusty kiss.

Men whistled and hooted while women wiped away tears.

Meanwhile, Loch looked on with bemusement. The lad was young and talented, yet he'd thrown away his career for a lass. Now, instead of finishing his training to become a warrior, he'd spend his days serving ale and tossing out drunks.

And the strangest thing was that Tor looked happy about it. He faced the crowd now, his arm slung around Alison's shoulders, a big grin on his face.

"Join us at *The Craignure Inn*," a woman called out then. All gazes, including Loch's, swiveled to where Mairi stood amongst the crowd. Her high cheekbones flushed slightly at having the attention of all upon her, yet her full lips curved in a welcoming smile. "I've prepared the happy couple a wedding feast, and we would like to share it with ye all." She paused then, her smile widening. "And while ye're at the inn, I invite ye to take a look around our new wing ... it was completed yesterday and is now ready for our first guests!"

A roar of approval went up at this invitation.

Loch's belly clenched hard. Lord, how he wanted her to smile at *him* again, as she once had. But it was as if he were invisible now. Caught up in the tide of well-wishers making their way back to Craignure, Mairi turned and made her way out of the castle courtyard.

Loch unclenched his hands from his sides, flexing them.

"Are ye not joining us, Loch?" Jack asked. His cousin had been following the others toward the gate but halted now and glanced over his shoulder. Beside him, Finn also stopped and looked back at Loch expectantly.

Loch shook his head.

Mairi wouldn't want him there, and he'd respect her wishes.

"Go on ahead," he said, waving them away. "I shall join ye later." He wouldn't, although once the lads had downed a few tankards of ale, they wouldn't care. Loch turned to where Astrid stood silently at his side. "Ye look like ye could do with warming yerself up, lass." Indeed, his sister looked haggard this afternoon. "Shall we take a cup of mulled wine together in my solar?"

Astrid gave a listless nod. She moved away from his side then, heading back toward the keep. But she'd only gone a few strides when her legs went from under her, and she crumpled like a newborn foal upon the cobbles.

A heartbeat later, Loch was there, scooping her up. Lord, she was as light as a bairn; there was nothing to her at all. He peered down at his sister's face, alarmed when her head rolled back. Astrid's eyes were closed, and her lips slightly parted. Her face was bloodless.

"What's wrong?" Jack was at his side then, his expression grim.

"I don't know," Loch muttered, even as foreboding clenched deep in his chest. His gaze met his cousin's. "Fetch the healer from the village while I carry her upstairs."

Standing beside his sister's bed, Loch watched silently as Donn, the healer who lived outside the castle walls, tended to Astrid.

The man was getting on in years, yet his hands were still steady. His weathered, sharp-featured face was creased with concern.

"Are ye in pain, Lady Astrid?" the healer asked as he gently palpitated her belly.

"No," she said huskily. "I came over all weak … I'm sure it will pass."

"Do ye feel any nausea?"

She shook her head.

"Any pain in yer chest?"

"No."

Donn placed a large palm on her forehead. "Ye don't appear to have a fever," he noted.

"No … but I *am* tired," Astrid replied. "And my limbs lack strength these days. It is a struggle to rouse myself from my bed in the mornings."

Loch frowned at this admission. It was hardly surprising since the lass picked at her food like a sparrow. He should have insisted she eat more.

After Donn had finished checking Astrid, he and Loch departed her chamber. Loch ushered the healer into his solar and shut the door. "What ails her?" he asked.

"I'm not sure," Donn admitted, his brow furrowing.

Loch folded his arms across his chest. "Ye must have a theory?"

The healer rubbed at his chin, eyeing Loch warily. "Aye … but ye won't like it."

Loch scowled. "Speak, man."

Donn gave a deep sigh. "I saw someone like this … years ago," he admitted after a brief pause. "A widow who lost her beloved husband. She pined terribly for him and wasted away before everyone's eyes."

Loch's heart slammed against his breastbone. "But Astrid isn't grieving anyone?"

"No," Donn replied slowly, cautious now. "But she did lose her father recently … and it's common knowledge that she's against her coming marriage."

Loch stiffened. There was no veiled criticism in the healer's voice, yet he felt judged, nonetheless. "She will rally, I'm sure," he replied after a brittle pause.

Donn nodded, even as his gaze remained uncertain. “Make sure she eats and drinks … Lady Astrid needs to regain her strength.”

“I will,” Loch assured him. Indeed, he’d sit with Astrid at mealtimes and feed her himself if necessary. Seeing his fiery sister so fragile roused strange and unwelcome emotions. A fierce protectiveness surged up inside him.

Donn made for the door. “I shall return tomorrow to check on her.”

“The widow ye spoke of,” Loch called out then. “Did she recover from her strange malady?”

The healer halted and turned to him. His sharp-featured face tightened, and he shook his head. “I did all that I could but to no avail,” he murmured. “Sometimes, there’s no mending a broken heart.”

25: PROUD TO CALL YE MY SON

ON THE FIFTH evening after Astrid had fallen ill, Loch sat by his sister's side watching her sleep.

Her breast rose and fell shallowly. Astrid lay so still, it was as if she were already half-dead—as if she'd merely given up on living. If this continued, she would surely die.

Dread wreathed up through Loch like dawn mist.

He'd hoped his sister's condition would improve with the passing of the days, yet it hadn't. He'd sat with her at each mealtime, presenting her with choice morsels, but she had no appetite at all. Eating made her bilious. As promised, Donn visited daily, although there was little the healer could do.

Astrid had taken to her bed and only rose from it to use the chamber pot. After a few days, she'd needed her maid's assistance to do even that.

His sister was wasting away before his eyes.

Loch's throat tightened then. *I did this to her.* Swallowing hard, he tried to shift the guilt that had settled like an anvil on his chest, but he couldn't. The alliance with the Mackinnons was important, not just to him but to his clan. He'd had the chance to turn things around, to bring peace to this isle.

But he hadn't expected to pay such a dear price.

Plenty of clan-chief's daughters were promised to rivals to secure alliances. It was the way of things—Astrid should have understood that, but his sister was far more sensitive than he'd realized. In pledging her to their clan's enemy and thwarting all her attempts to get out of it, he'd somehow broken her spirit.

Loch leaned forward then and placed his hand over Astrid's. Her fingers were so fragile and cold. She didn't stir under his touch, and the pressure on his breastbone increased.

Guilt dug its claws into him then. *Ye can't let this go on,* it needled him. *Ye need to do something ... before it's too late.*

Dragging a hand down his face, Loch rose from his stool. He was waging a war with himself tonight. Curse it, he was still reluctant to give up on the peace he'd agreed with their rivals. Kendric Mackinnon would want the wife he'd been promised.

Leaving his sister sleeping, Loch let himself quietly out of her chamber. He then took the hallway back to his solar. Luag was there, as always, curled by the fire. The wolfhound looked up as the laird strode in, favoring him with an adoring gaze.

"Don't look at me like that, lad," Loch grumbled, heading for the sideboard. "I don't deserve it."

Pouring himself a generous cup of elderberry wine, he slugged back a large gulp and glanced over at his dog once more. "Any ideas on how I can rouse Astrid from her misery?"

Luag whined in response, and Loch sighed. "I didn't think so."

Instead of retiring to his chair by the fire, as he usually did at this hour, he carried his cup of wine and a lantern over to his desk. It was drafty by the window, even with the sacking lowered. Now that they were marching through December, the weather had turned icy. The first snow wouldn't be far away.

Staring down at the ledger he'd left open on the desk, Loch took another gulp of wine. He was behind with the accounts. Astrid had taken most of his attention over the past few days. It had been difficult to concentrate on anything else.

The lantern cast a ruddy glow over the piles of parchment and ledgers stacked around the edges of the large desk. He still hadn't cleared them all away.

Still standing, Loch cast an eye over the papers. Perhaps he could sort through some of them now. It would distract him from worries about his sister—and from difficult decisions he knew were looming.

There were a few old accounts ledgers here that could be shelved, and several missives from various chieftains and clan-chiefs, not just upon the Isle of Mull but throughout the Highlands. There were some letters from Tormod MacLeod upon the Isle of Skye to his father. Of course, the Macleans and the Macleods were strong allies and had called upon each other in times of need.

Loch's brow furrowed as he skimmed through some of the missives. Tormod was a very old man these days. In one of the letters, he jested that his white beard was so long that he could tuck it into his girdle. Soon, his son Malcolm would succeed him.

Loch would do well to write to Tormod while he still lived, to assure him that the old friendship between their clans thrived.

Lowering himself to the chair behind the desk, Loch set down his cup of wine, took a quill from its holder, and dipped it into a pot of ink. He then scribbled a note to himself to ensure he didn't forget to contact the Macleods.

He replaced the quill, staring moodily at the letters he'd been reading. His gaze slid then to the folded parchment, sealed in wax, that still sat upon the desk—waiting for him.

Reaching out, tracing the familiar seal with his fingertip, his gaze lingered on his name. Standing up, he then carried the letter over to the fireplace, placing it on the mantelpiece. He glanced down at where Luag had pushed himself up against his legs. "What do ye think, lad?" he murmured, reaching down to stroke the wolfhound's ears. "Should I open it?"

As expected, Luag had no answer for him.

Picking up the parchment once more, Loch's mouth pursed. "Maybe I should toss the cursed thing in the fire," he muttered. "Save myself the old man's final tirade."

However, he didn't.

Moments passed as he turned the missive over a few times in his hands before he set his jaw, broke the seal, and opened the letter. Then, he began to read.

Greetings to my dearest son, Loch Maclean, from Iain Maclean, clan-chief and laird of Duart Castle upon the Isle of Mull.

It was a convoluted salutation, yet typical of such missives, even amongst kin. All the same, seeing his father's familiar slanted handwriting made something tug deep in his chest. Exhaling sharply, Loch continued reading.

I hope this letter finds ye well, my son, and that ye have returned to us healthy and unmaimed after serving our king. Many years have passed since ye sailed away from Mull, and yet it sometimes feels as if ye departed just yesterday. Ye will find as ye grow older that time passes with increasing swiftness.

Ye might think that we are isolated here, upon this lonely isle, and that little of what happens on the mainland reaches my ears, yet I have kept abreast of yer movements. I learned that ye were with the Bruce at Loudon Hill, and that ye helped him plunder the north of England in the years that followed. Word reached me that ye were with our king for his victory at Bannockburn too this year. I learned of how ye led yer men into the heart of it all, how ye shouted our battle cry as ye clove a path through the English.

Death or victory.

I must confess that tears sprang to my ears to hear such news. I am proud to call ye my son. Proud that ye carried our banner far and wide.

Loch stopped reading a moment, an ache rising in his throat. Suddenly, he didn't want to continue. It was too raw, too intimate—he could almost hear the rough timbre of his father's voice, as if he were sitting next to him.

Swallowing, he tightened his grip on the letter and forced himself on.

I am dying.

This morning, I awoke with pain down my left side, and as I write this, I feel strangely weak and nausea bites at my throat. Something is wrong.

To many, I am still the man I was, yet I have not felt myself since I buried yer mother five years ago. Something changed within me, a breaking of sorts, and I have not managed to put myself back together.

Gellise was my strength, my reason to rise from my bed in the mornings, and without her, I find myself crumbling into ruin. My body grows weary, and the strength leaches out of my limbs. These days, even climbing a flight of stairs leaves me weak and breathless. Only Astrid knows that I'm ailing—her and Donn the healer. I have sworn them both to secrecy.

Ye will likely find such confessions weak, yet by the time ye read this, I will be fodder for the worms. As the end nears, my pride matters less to me than it once did.

Ye are strong, lad. Ye never needed any of us, least of all a bull-headed father who tried to mold ye into his image.

I tried to change ye, and for that I am sorry.

That is why ye stayed away for so long, I am sure of it, but one day, ye will find yerself back upon Mull, and ye will wear my ring and pick up the torch I have left burning, waiting for ye.

To rule Duart is yer birthright, yer calling.

After my passing, Kendric Mackinnon is likely to try and make an accord with our clan. I will not be there to counsel ye, but I urge ye not to take him at his word. The man is a smiling assassin and cannot be trusted.

Live well, my son, and look after yer sister. She is more fragile than she appears.

Farewell, Loch.
Yer loving father.

Loch put down the letter and touched the signet ring he wore upon the little finger of his right hand.

Memories washed over him now. For years, he'd focused on all the things that vexed him about his father, for they'd clashed constantly in the months preceding Loch's call to arms. But reading this letter, which had come from the heart, unlocked flashes of other, happier, times.

His father teaching him to ride his first pony.

Perching on his knee at Yule as a bairn and pestering him for a sip of mulled wine.

The earthy rumble of Iain Maclean's laughter at mealtimes.

Sparring with him in the outer courtyard. His father goading him with a grin, telling him not to strike so high, to pay more attention to his opponent rather than rushing in with hot-headed zeal.

Loch closed his eyes, trying to ward off the memories, yet they flooded over him.

His hand clenched around the letter he still held.

Aye, he'd won honor and glory in battle, but Iain Maclean was the better man. Big-hearted and honest, he'd known how to give of himself, how to love.

He'd also found a peace within himself that had always eluded his son.

Tears burned the back of Loch's eyelids, and his throat started to ache. He twisted the signet ring, hard.

His father had gone to his grave proud of his only son. He'd died still loving him, despite that Loch had given him *nothing* over the years.

Instead of rejecting everything the old man had to say, he could have learned from him. His father's letter had held up a looking glass, and it wasn't easy to look at what it showed him.

All the insults his sister, and Mairi, had thrown at him over the past weeks, suddenly hit home. This evening, he no longer wore his armor, and the blades sank deep.

He was self-centered and vainglorious.

He was callous and careless with the feelings of those who cared for him.

The truth was that he wouldn't soothe the uneasiness within him by forcing his sister to wed his enemy, or by treating his leannan thoughtlessly. Over the years, he'd either taken love for granted or treated it with contempt—but things had to change.

If he continued down this path, he deserved to die a lonely, bitter man.

26: FROM THE HEART

MAIRI TIPPED HER head back and let the snowflakes land upon her face.

It was her ritual every winter, and it usually made her smile—but not this morning.

Ever since her confrontation with Loch, she'd congratulated herself on how well she was doing. It had been liberating to stand up for herself, to finally put a stop to a relationship that had been slowly eroding her self-worth ever since Loch's return to Mull. Aye, he'd left her with no choice in the end.

Yet at the same time, there was a yawning emptiness inside her now—a chasm that no amount of rationalization or good sense could fill. Loch Maclean wasn't good for her, but she'd always love him. And she knew, without a doubt, that there would be no one else for her.

Trying to ignore the dull ache in her chest, Mairi closed her eyes. The delicate tickle of snow on her face was pleasant, and she sighed.

"I don't know why ye like snow so much," Alison grumbled next to her. "It merely *vexes* me."

Mairi glanced over at her cousin. Indeed, Alison did look cross this morning. Her nose was red-tipped, and she was huddled within the folds of her woolen cloak.

"It's not just the snow I like," she reminded Alison. "But winter too."

The two women were walking amongst the market stalls on the docks. The aroma of hot mutton pies wafted through the gelid air, and a crowd gathered around the ruddy-faced woman selling them.

There was no fish for sale today, no men hauling in their catch, or mending nets on the sand beside the jetty. The fishing boats had been pulled high upon the beach and were now covered in snow. Nonetheless, the smokehouse a few yards away on the waterfront was doing a good trade this morning. As she drew nearer to the shop, Mairi inhaled the pungent smell of smoked herring.

It was the Yuletide Eve market, and she had a busy day ahead, for she'd be cooking for the host of locals who flocked to *The Craignure Inn* every Yuletide. Perhaps she'd purchase some smoked fish on the way home, to serve with crusty bread and freshly churned butter, alongside the usual roast goose. She loved Yule and all the traditions surrounding it. Focusing on the celebrations took the edge off her heartache.

It was a reminder that life moved on, and she had to try and do the same.

She wouldn't let Loch break her.

"I love the moody skies, the way the sea whips itself up into a frenzy," Mairi elaborated after a brief pause. "The beauty of snow and ice … and how cold it is outdoors at Yuletide while inside we warm ourselves before a roaring hearth. There's a wonder to it all, don't ye think?"

Alison snorted. "If ye say so … I, for one, am counting the days until the first of March."

"Ye can," Mairi replied with a rueful shake of her head. "But meanwhile, ye are wishing away time." She managed a tight smile then. "Da always warned me it was foolish to do that."

The cousins' gazes met, and Alison's mouth quirked. "Uncle Athol was a wise one," she murmured. She looped her arm through Mairi's then. "Very well … I will do my best not to grumble too much about my chilblains and numb fingers and toes."

"That's a relief to hear … the whining does get on my nerves at times."

Alison dug her in the ribs with a sharp elbow. "I do not whine!"

Flashing her cousin an arch look, Mairi stopped before an egg vendor. The woman hunched there, under a snow-encrusted awning, flashed her a wide smile. Of course, she knew Mairi was her best customer.

"Two dozen eggs please, Ana," Mairi greeted her.

"Aye." The woman took the basket Mairi handed her and started to fill it. "Will ye be making yer famous honey and dried plum cakes again this year?"

"Of course," Mairi assured her. "I'll also be making apple tarts and egg custards." Her throat thickened then. "I want this Yule to be special ... in my Da's honor."

Ana's eyes misted. "What a bonnie idea. I shall make sure Angus and I join ye for the Yuletide feast tomorrow then."

"And ye will be more than welcome, as always," Mairi replied huskily.

Once the basket was filled and Mairi had handed over a penny, she moved on. Alison stepped close then. Like Ana's, her eyes gleamed with emotion. "Ye look so sad these days," she murmured. "I wish ye'd give a *real* smile."

Mairi reached out her free hand and squeezed her cousin's arm. "Don't mind me, Ali. I'll rally ... I always do."

"Hosting Yule in Uncle Athol's honor is a lovely gesture" —Alison favored Mairi with a wistful smile—"although the celebrations won't be the same without him." Her gaze lingered upon her face. Alison was no fool. She knew the bittersweet memories that Yuletide brought weren't the only reason for her cousin's low mood.

"No, they won't be ... but this was the best way I could think of to keep him close."

Wordlessly, Alison put an arm around her waist and squeezed tight. Mairi hugged her back. "Come on," Mairi murmured, after a short spell. "Let's get the rest of our shopping done ... before the best things have gone."

Side by side, the cousins continued through the snowy market, buying onions, carrots, and a bag of chestnuts.

However, Mairi was haggling with a man selling freshly slaughtered geese—for she intended to spit-roast four over a fire the following day—when she spied a familiar figure wending his way through the press of shoppers.

She froze, halting mid-sentence.

Loch Maclean always stood out in a crowd, and today was no exception. He wore a fine woolen cloak, edged in snowy ermine.

"Mairi?" Alison was tugging at her sleeve now. "Will ye take four geese for three silver pennies?"

Mairi jolted and dragged her attention away from the laird, who'd seen her and was now heading her way. "Two and a half," she muttered. "The geese aren't as fat as last year."

"Aye, they are!" The vendor protested, puffing out his chest.

"Two and a half," Mairi repeated, her tone turning steely now. "Don't take me for a fool, Finlay. Ye know the geese aren't worth more than that."

Finlay's eyes widened, and they locked gazes for a few long moments, before he pursed his lips and nodded. "All right then."

"Good morning, Mairi ... Alison."

The rumble of Loch's voice wrapped itself around Mairi. She ignored him for a few moments, concentrating instead on handing the coins over to Finlay. The man then set about stuffing the four geese into sacks. Mairi and Alison would have the lengthy chore later of gutting and plucking the birds ready to be roasted the following morning.

"Greetings, Maclean," Alison spoke first, her tone polite yet uncharacteristically reserved. "What brings ye to market on such a snowy morning?"

"I promised my sister we'd have chestnuts in the stuffing with the roast pork this eve," he replied. "And I don't wish to disappoint her."

Something in his tone made Mairi glance his way.

Loch had been looking at Alison, yet the moment Mairi turned her attention upon him, his gaze shifted to her. His expression was serious this morning, despite the festive cheer of the men and women who bustled around them.

White snowflakes settled upon his dark hair and the shoulders of his fine ermine-trimmed cloak. One or two even frosted his long dark eyelashes.

"I heard Lady Astrid was unwell," Mairi said, wishing her voice wasn't quite so husky when she addressed him.

"She was," he replied softly.

"What ailed her?" Alison asked. It was a bold question, but Mairi's cousin wasn't one to shy from difficult subjects.

"A melancholy of sorts," Loch replied. "One that made her waste away." He swallowed then. "I nearly lost her."

"But she has rallied?" Mairi asked, alarm fluttering through her at this news. With all the activity of getting ready for Yuletide, she hadn't realized Lady Astrid's condition had been so grave.

Loch nodded. "I broke off her betrothal to Kendric Mackinnon ... and with each day, she gains strength." His night-brown eyes darkened then. "I shouldn't have forced her into a marriage she didn't want ... I realize that now."

Mairi didn't reply immediately. In truth, his admission caught her off guard. She wouldn't have expected Loch to break such a promise to the Mackinnons, or for him to admit he was in the wrong.

"How did the Mackinnon answer ye?" she asked after a pause.

His mouth lifted at the edges. "He hasn't responded to my missive yet ... but I'm sure he will."

An awkward silence fell then as they regarded each other.

Alison was the first to speak, shattering the tension. "Ye do realize that thumbing yer nose at the Mackinnon like this will only make ye even more of a hero to yer clansmen?"

Loch shifted his attention to Alison and raised an inquiring eyebrow. "How so?"

"Ye got yer cattle and yer land back, and then broke yer promise," she replied. "They'll all think ye did it for revenge, for everything he's put the folk of these lands through over the years. And they'll love ye for it."

Loch gave a soft snort. "I hadn't looked at it that way."

“The people here all—”

Mairi cleared her throat, interrupting them. This conversation was dragging on too long for her liking. “Aye, well ... I’m relieved to hear that yer sister is recovering,” she said pointedly, casting her cousin a warning glance. “Please pass on our best wishes to Lady Astrid.”

Loch took the hint. “I will.” He stepped back, nodding politely to the two women. “I shall let ye continue with yer shopping ... I wish ye both a bonnie ‘Long Night’.”

“And ye,” Mairi replied.

Loch turned, moving away through the crowd.

Mairi watched him go.

“By the Saints,” Alison murmured. “The laird seems ... subdued.”

“Aye,” Mairi agreed, tearing her gaze from Loch’s broad back. “No doubt, nearly losing his sister has made him reconsider some of his values.”

“Maybe Lady Astrid isn’t his only regret,” Alison suggested.

Mairi frowned at her cousin. Alison was loose with her tongue this morning—too loose. Finlay was watching their exchange with bright, curious eyes. After everything she’d weathered of late, the last thing she needed was the gossipmongers of Craignure to start whispering behind her back.

Not that there was anything to whisper about—not anymore.

“I raise this goblet ... my father’s finest cup ... to ye all, my loyal warriors and retainers. And I thank each of ye for yer fealty, for accepting me as yer laird.” Loch paused his speech, his gaze surveying the faces of those seated at the long trestle tables around him—the men, women, and bairns who resided within this castle.

His chest tightened then as he observed the smiles on their faces, the respect shining in their eyes. Alison Macquarie had spoken true: breaking his promise to the Mackinnon had only elevated him to a new status in their eyes.

When he'd returned from Craignure earlier in the day, passing through Duart village on his way up to the castle, the locals had poured out of their bothies to greet him—seemingly unconcerned that he had ruined their best chance for peace.

Loch held his goblet aloft. It gleamed in the light of the banks of candles adorning the great hall. The vessel was indeed beautiful, made of silver and studded with garnets and amber—a cup his father reserved for special occasions. After a brief pause, Loch continued. "I will strive to lead our clan to greatness again ... I swear it ... upon the memory of my father, Iain Maclean."

A thunderous applause of clapping and foot stomping followed, shaking the tables, and rattling the crockery.

Loch's skin prickled. He'd thought nothing could beat the thrill of victory after battle, yet he was wrong. Being surrounded by his clansmen was far better. "Death or victory!" he shouted.

"Death or victory!"

Tankards thumped against wood and more cheers and applause lifted into the rafters. Moments later, everyone fell upon the Yuletide Eve banquet. Indeed, there was roast suckling pig stuffed with chestnuts and apple; rich venison stew and dumplings, braised kale, and onions; and bread studded with walnuts. Huge wheels of cheese had also been carried out, and later, delicate fruit tarts would be served. It was a fine feast, and the following day, the cooks would do it all again.

Lowering himself to his carven seat, Loch took a sip from his goblet, savoring the rich, fruity bramble wine. Growing up, they'd always had bramble wine at Yule. His mother had made it every year, and this was her recipe.

"A rousing speech," Jack called from the opposite end of the clan-chief's table, flashing Loch a grin. "Ye might make a proper laird yet."

Loch pulled a face. "Idiot." He turned then to where his sister sat beside him and raised his goblet aloft once more. "Merry Yuletide, Astrid."

"And to ye, brother," she replied, her lips lifting at the edges. "That *was* a fine speech." Her brown eyes glistened then. "From the heart."

Loch's mouth curved. "Aye, well ... it was time." He paused then and studied her. Dressed in a fine purple surcote and lilac kirtle, his sister looked far healthier this eve. Astrid was still painfully thin, yet she'd lost her pallor and there was a faint blush of color to her cheeks, for it was warm in here. Nearby, the 'Yule log', a huge branch of oak, smoldered in the hearth, heating the large hall. "How are ye feeling?"

"Much better, thank ye," she answered.

Their gazes held, and Loch recalled how Astrid had sobbed with relief when he'd advised her that he'd sent off a missive to the Mackinnon, informing him that the wedding would no longer take place. He'd written the letter an hour after reading the missive his father had left him behind and had sent a fast rider away with it with the first blush of dawn.

Loch had taken her in his arms, holding her while she wept. His sister's gratitude felt like a stake to the heart though, reminding him that, in his ambition to forge peace at all costs, he'd mistreated her. He hoped to make it up to Astrid, but there was still a reserve between them in the days following. Of course, trust couldn't be won back by just one kind act. Their relationship would take time to mend.

Astrid's eyes glinted then, a smile creasing her face. "I see we have chestnut stuffing."

Loch's mouth quirked. "Aye ... I bought the last of them at Craignure market this morning." He leaned forward then and spooned some stuffing onto Astrid's trencher. The lass still ate like a mouse, yet at least she *was* eating these days.

"And walnut bread too," she added, reaching out and helping herself to a slice. "My favorite."

Loch's smile turned wistful. "It was Ma's as well," he murmured, surprised that he'd remembered the detail.

"Aye." Astrid's expression sobered, and she dropped her gaze to her trencher. "It's been five years … and I still miss her."

Loch's brow furrowed. In truth, over the years, he'd thought little about the woman who'd birthed him, the woman who'd worried over him when he was sick or hurt. What a knave he'd been.

"I haven't been to the kirkyard to visit her or Da yet," he admitted gruffly after a lengthy pause. "Shall we go there on Saint Stephen's? There will still be snow, but we can lay wreaths on their graves … if ye like?"

Astrid raised her chin, and when her gaze met his, her eyes gleamed with unshed tears. "Aye, Loch," she replied softly. "I'd like that very much."

27: THE THINGS THAT REALLY MATTER

"THOSE WERE THE finest honey cakes I have ever eaten ... and the rest of it wasn't bad either."

The edges of Mairi's lips lifted as she looked down at the elderly man and removed his empty trencher. "That's quite a compliment, Aaron."

He flashed her a gummy smile. "Aye, lass ... now what about a nice wee cup of mulled wine to finish the meal off?"

Mairi nodded. Straightening up, she cast her gaze around the common room. Boughs of ivy draped from the rafters, and holly wreaths hung from the pitted stone walls. Contented faces, cheeks ruddy from the warmth of the fire and too much rich food and drink, looked back at her. "A round of mulled wine for all?"

"Aye," everyone chorused.

Keeping her smile in place, even as weariness dragged at her, Mairi shifted her attention to where Alison and Tor were clearing up. It had been a good day, full of festive cheer and warmth. Mairi had thrown herself into the celebrations, yet she longed to retire now and keep her own company for a spell.

"Ye'd better finish up here," she murmured to her cousin, "While I see to the wine."

"Off ye go then," Alison replied with a wink. "They're all waiting."

"Aye," Todd added with a grin. "All that good food has made them thirsty."

"It's just as well I ordered in extra wine," Mairi replied with a rueful shake of her head. "Or they'd drink me dry."

"Do ye need me to roll out another barrel?" Tor asked.

Mairi shook her head, flashing him a grateful smile. "There's enough left ... but thank ye, all the same."

Tor's presence at *The Craignure Inn* was welcome indeed. The patrons behaved themselves better with him here, and he worked hard too, which was a boon at Yuletide.

The inn's common room was packed to the rafters today. As planned, Mairi had served smoked herrings, roast geese, and a selection of roasted and braised vegetables for the Yule feast. Afterward, they'd feasted on a selection of sweet treats. The revelry had drawn out throughout the afternoon—and dusk had recently settled outside—yet everyone was having such a good time that no one showed any signs of moving on.

"Play yer whistle for us, Tor!" One of the patrons called out then.

"Aye," another chorused. "A bonnie Yuletide tune!"

"He will," Alison promised. "Just as soon as we've tidied up a bit." She winked at her husband then, and he smiled back.

Mairi's ribs constricted at the love in Tor's eyes as he looked upon his wife.

How must it feel to be so adored, cherished?

Banishing the thought, and chiding herself for being such a goose, Mairi retreated to the kitchen. She then set about mulling more plum wine in the cauldron that hung over the hearth. As the wine warmed, she added some costly cloves and shards of cinnamon bark she'd bought from a merchant two years earlier. The spices were so expensive and difficult to get hold of that she only ever used them at Yuletide.

A heavy sigh escaped Mairi then. She'd kept going all day, with a dogged determination not to let sadness in. However, tiredness had lowered her defenses. She couldn't retreat upstairs though—not yet. There was still work to be done.

It didn't take long for the scent of mulled wine to fill the kitchen. When it was ready, Mairi ladled the hot spiced wine into two earthen jugs and carried them into the common room.

She'd just entered when her gaze alighted on three men hanging up their cloaks by the door.

Shaking snow out of his hair, Loch turned, his gaze spearing hers across the crowded room.

"Merry Yuletide, Mairi!" Jack called out from behind the laird, flashing her a roguish grin. "We're in time for mulled wine, I hear."

He and Finn followed Loch to where some men seated by the fire hurriedly made room for them at their table.

Mairi drew in a deep breath. *Ye can do this*. She could serve Loch Maclean mulled wine and honey cakes in a professional manner—she had to get used to him frequenting the inn. "Aye," she replied. "Take a seat."

Doing her best to keep her expression serene, even as her pulse drummed in her ears, Mairi started to make her way around the tables, pouring wine into cups. Meanwhile, Alison went back into the kitchen to retrieve some honey cakes for their late-coming guests.

"Yuletide blessings to ye all," she greeted Loch, Jack, and Finn politely, careful to avoid the laird's eye.

"And to ye, Mairi," Loch replied, speaking for the first time. "Have ye had a good day?"

"Aye ... although it's been the busiest Yule in a long while," Mairi silently cursed the way her hand trembled as she poured his wine. "Tor's help is welcome indeed ... I don't know how we coped without him."

"We miss the lad's presence at Duart," Loch replied. "But this is the path he has chosen ... and it's a wise one."

Finn snorted as he pulled out the pouch of knucklebones he took everywhere. "Wise? The lad gave up a life dedicated to the sword and glory ... to serve ale." He shot Mairi an apologetic look. "Sorry, no insult intended."

Mairi shrugged. "None taken."

"The sword and glory aren't everything, Finn," Loch said quietly.

Finn cast his friend a sidelong glance and poured the knucklebones out onto the table. “Aren’t they?”

Jack smirked. “They won’t keep ye warm at night, for one thing.”

“I don’t know about that,” Finn answered with a sly grin. “There’s plenty a lass keen for a tumble with a man who’s proved his valor.” He glanced over at Mairi then, his mirth fading. “Sorry, Mairi.”

“Ye can stop apologizing,” she muttered. “I work in an inn … I’ve heard far coarser comments.”

“Even so, Finn should remember his manners around ye,” Loch said. He was frowning now, although not at her but his friend.

Around them, men at some of the nearby tables were also viewing Finn MacDonald with narrow-eyed looks—although there was resentment in their eyes rather than displeasure. Even three months after their return, many locals still harbored a grudge against him.

But Finn paid the unfriendly stares no mind. He merely favored Loch with a shrug.

“Enjoy yer wine,” Mairi said, stepping back. She then turned and moved on to the next table.

And as she went, she felt Loch’s gaze follow her.

“Ye should really stop staring at the lass.”

“Aye … either go over and talk to Mairi or put yer eyeballs back in yer skull and join us at knucklebones.”

Loch cut his gaze away from where he’d been watching Mairi talk to Alison by the bench near the kitchen door and scowled at his two companions—both of whom were favoring him with knowing looks. “Mind yer own business,” he growled.

“I think not,” Jack taunted him. “Not when *yer* business is far more intriguing.” He then rattled the knucklebones he held in his palm and grinned at Finn. “Ready to go again?”

“Aye,” Finn replied, although his gaze narrowed as he viewed Loch. “What’s come over ye of late?”

Loch stiffened. “Nothing.”

Finn pulled a face. “Liar. First ye break yer faith with the Mackinnon and then—”

“And just as well he did too,” Jack cut in, frowning. “Although there’s still a reckoning to be had with that bastard.”

Finn ignored him. Both he and Loch were used to hearing Jack mutter such threats. “And then ye start making passionate speeches and swearing oaths on yer old man’s memory,” he continued. “I thought ye didn’t have any time for him?”

“I didn’t,” Loch replied, picking up his cup of mulled wine and taking a sip. “But I was wrong.” He paused then, wondering whether to confide in them before deciding he would. “Da left me a letter.”

Jack inclined his head. “He did?”

“Aye ... he knew he was dying and wrote to me. I saw the sealed missive shortly after we arrived back at Duart, but I’ve only just opened it.”

“What took ye so long?” Finn asked.

“I don’t know.” Loch’s mouth twisted. “Laziness, selfishness ... cowardice.”

Both Finn and Jack stilled at this proclamation.

“Ye’re no coward,” Jack said quietly, discomfort flickering across his features.

“I *am*,” Loch corrected him. His gaze flicked to Mairi, who was now moving toward the kitchen. “About the things that matter.”

An awkward silence fell at the table, and Loch made no effort to fill it.

He was in a reckless mood tonight. The past days had ripped him open. Now that he’d seen the truth about himself, there was no unseeing it—no going back to his old ways.

Jack and Finn had no response to his admission, and after a while, they resumed their game of knucklebones, helping themselves to the honey cakes Alison had brought them earlier.

Loch didn’t touch the cakes. His stomach had closed. Instead, he nursed his mulled wine and waited for Mairi to emerge from the kitchen. And when she did, two more jugs of mulled wine in hand, his gaze tracked her across the floor.

She was lovelier than ever this eve. Her cheeks were flushed, her eyes bright. She'd be tired, after working the busiest day of the year, but she still carried herself proudly. There was an elegance to her movements that he'd always admired—in truth, there were many things he admired about Mairi Macquarie.

Her strength. Her guileless nature. Her warm heart.

And yet he'd never told her.

Setting his cup down, Loch pushed himself up from the table.

Jack glanced up. "Where are ye off to?"

Loch ignored him. Moving away from the table, he walked across the floor to where Mairi had just filled the last of the waiting cups. An elderly man was thanking her.

"Mairi."

Setting the jugs down, she turned. Unsurprisingly, her expression was veiled, wary, as she viewed him. "Aye?"

Loch stared down at her, his pulse racing now. He could have made this easier on himself—he could have waited until the common room was empty before he approached Mairi—but he didn't deserve to have things easy.

And Mairi needed to hear these words now, with everyone as her witness.

Even so, he hesitated.

Satan's cods, he was fearless on the battlefield but broke out in a cold sweat at the thought of making himself vulnerable with this woman.

Loch rode the fear out, even as he clenched his hands by his sides. Moments passed, and Mairi's expression turned quizzical. The rise and fall of surrounding conversation died away then, and the common room fell silent.

All eyes were on him now.

Loch had to make this moment count. Drawing in a deep, steadying breath, he lowered himself onto one knee in front of Mairi.

Her gaze snapped wide. “Loch,” she gasped. “What are ye—”

“I’m apologizing to ye, lass,” he replied, his voice developing a hoarse edge. “For not letting ye into my heart all those years ago … for leaving ye as I did, with a promise I forgot the moment Mull disappeared on the horizon … and for never sending word while I was away.” He paused there, tipping his head back as he continued to hold her eye. Mairi frowned, and an ache rose under his breastbone. Curse it, the words sounded hollow. They weren’t enough.

A deep flush had risen to Mairi’s cheeks, and her face was strained. “Get up,” she muttered. “Everyone’s staring.”

“Let them,” Loch growled.

28: MY HEART IS YERS FOREVER

"I'M SORRY TOO, for how I treated ye upon my return to the isle," Loch continued, even as the blood roared in his ears, "for not keeping my word ... for behaving as if ye don't matter. The truth is ye *do* matter to me ... more than I have words to express."

Mairi's lips parted, her tawny eyes shadowing.

The ache in Loch's chest twisted hard. "Ye are a goddess, Mairi Macquarie," he rasped. "And ye are right ... ye were always too good for me." She sucked in a sharp inhale at this admission. However, Loch plowed on. "But that doesn't mean I want another man to have ye. I'm a selfish bastard, but for *ye,* I'd strive to be a better man. I'd worship ye as ye truly deserve, and for ye, I'd tear myself open and give ye the parts of me I've guarded for too long."

Mairi wore a stunned expression now as if she couldn't believe her ears. She likely thought a changeling knelt before her, one who'd taken the laird's form. The man he used to be wouldn't have prostrated himself like this. Once, he'd have sneered at the sight of someone making such a fool of himself.

"Life has no shine without ye, lass," he admitted then, his voice roughening further. "My title, my castle, my lands ... are all meaningless." He broke off then, swallowing in an attempt to dislodge the lump that had risen in his throat. "Aye, that's the truth of it, mo chridhe," he whispered. "I love ye ... and if ye would allow it, I'd make ye my wife."

Silence followed these words.

Mairi continued to stare at him, her chest rising and falling sharply now. "Loch," she finally managed, her voice strangled. "Don't play games with me."

"This is no game, lass." He reached up and took her hands, squeezing firmly. "I'm in earnest. Be my wife, Lady Maclean of Duart Castle, and rule at my side." He paused then, fear that she'd reject him cramping his stomach. "*Please*."

Mairi remained silent, her eyes glittering with tears now. He could see she was still struggling with this. He needed to find a way to convince her.

Still clasping her hands, Loch rose to his feet and cast his gaze around the room. Everyone was staring at him with bemused or stunned expressions. "I wish to take Mairie Macquarie as my wife," he announced. "Does anyone here take issue with that?"

A beat followed before a chorus of 'no' and a flurry of shaking heads ensued.

Loch turned back to Mairi, stepping close and squeezing her hands tight. "See, my love," he said huskily. "Everyone here gives us their blessing."

Mairi cleared her throat. "That's because they're all scared of ye."

Loch gave a soft snort. "Good." He raised a hand then, his fingers brushing away a tear that had escaped and was now rolling down her cheek. "Just as long as *ye* don't fear me." He swallowed hard. "Please forgive me, and give me a chance to prove myself. My word is good this time, lass. I swear it."

Mairi inhaled slowly, trying to fight the whirlpool of emotion that was dragging her into its vortex.

Lord, she'd told herself she would no longer believe a word that came out of Loch Maclean's mouth. She'd vowed she wouldn't let him weave a sensual enchantment around her ever again. But she'd never expected him to sink to one knee before her, for him to lay himself bare the way he just had, to admit such things before a room full of onlookers.

And now, he'd asked her to marry him and dared anyone to challenge his decision.

Eventually, she drew in a deep, shaky breath. "Well then … I can't argue with that … can I?"

A tender smile curved Loch's lips as he shook his head. "S ann leatsa a tha mo chridhe gu bràth," he whispered, his eyes glistening.

My heart is yers forever.

The whirlpool sucked her into its depths then, and Mairi's hard-won composure crumbled. She raised her hands, covering her face, as sobs twisted up. It was too much. She wasn't strong enough to withstand this storm.

Murmuring an endearment, Loch drew her into his arms and cradled her close as she wept against his chest.

"I have ye, lass," he murmured.

Eventually, the tempest of sobs eased, and Mairi raised her head. She likely looked a fright, with a blotchy face and swollen eyes, yet Loch gazed down at her as if she was the bonniest thing he'd ever seen.

The love that glowed in his eyes made her breathing hitch.

Aye, he'd spoken honestly. He did love her.

"Well then," Alison spoke up, her voice tight with emotion and impatience. "How much longer will ye keep us all hanging? Will ye wed him or not?"

Mairi glanced her cousin's way. Alison's heart-shaped face was wet with tears. Tor stood with her, his arm protectively slung about her shoulders, his expression expectant.

"Aye," auld Aaron piped up behind her. "What will it be, lass?"

Mairi raised her attention to Loch's face once more, joy unfurling in her breast. "Aye," she whispered. "I am yers, Loch."

A wide smile stretched his face, even as tears glittered upon his eyelashes. He gave a whoop then and lifted her off the ground, whirling her around.

Mairi let out a squeal and raised her arms, wrapping them around his neck.

Loch set her down, and she kissed him, feverishly. He responded in kind, his mouth devouring hers. They embraced where they stood, uncaring of their audience.

Meanwhile, the common room erupted with cheering and applause.

Lifting her mouth from Loch's, Mairi traced her lips across his bearded cheek to the shell of his ear. "Take me upstairs," she whispered. "And *show* me that yer word is good."

"Aye," he said roughly. "Ye need not ask twice."

Loch scooped her up into his arms, turned, and carried her across the floor toward the stairs. His gaze never left Mairi's face, and the intensity of it made her shiver, despite the warmth inside the common room.

"Don't worry about the rest of us," Alison called after them. Mairi peeked over Loch's shoulder to see that her cousin wore a wicked grin. "We'll finish cleaning up."

Mairi mouthed 'thank ye'.

Moments later, Loch was climbing the creaky wooden stairs, and as soon as they were out of view of the common room, Mairi kissed him again, her tongue mating with his. Loch made it to the landing before striding down the narrow hallway above, to her chamber. He yanked the door open and carried her inside, kicking it shut behind him.

And then they were on each other, their kisses frenzied now.

Mairi tore at his clothing, and he wrenched at hers. The sound of rending fabric echoed through the chamber, blending with the crackling of the hearth. It wasn't as stuffy in here as the common room downstairs, yet the air that caressed Mairi's naked skin was warm.

However, when they both were naked, Loch took a step back. Breathing hard, he gazed upon her, studying every inch of her body as if seeing it for the first time.

"Ye have seen me in nothing but my skin before, ye know?" Mairi teased, her voice rough with want.

"Aye," he rasped, "but this time, I want to fully appreciate ye ... to tell ye how lovely ye are. How it almost hurts me to look upon ye."

Mairi's breathing caught, for the expression upon his face was fierce now.

Loch reached out, his fingers trailing down her jaw to her neck, and then down into the deep valley between her breasts. "Ye have a body as lovely as The Morrígan herself," he murmured. "Lush and strong ... soft and smooth ... and I will worship ye for the rest of my life." He lowered himself before her, his lips feathering across her breasts. He then drew a nipple deep into the heated cavern of his mouth and began to suckle her.

Mairi gave a soft cry and arched into him.

He spent a long while suckling each breast in turn, grazing each berry-hard nipple with his teeth, drawing the pleasure out until she tangled her fingers in his hair, until she gasped his name.

After that, he rose to his feet and drew her with him to the bed. There, he lay her down and spread her out before beginning a leisurely exploration of her body—and all the while, he whispered endearments and told her how beautiful she was, how much he loved her, wanted her.

His need for her was very much in evidence though, for his swollen shaft strained toward her as he licked, nibbled, and suckled his way down her body. His seed leaked from its crown, running down the engorged length of his erection. Yet Loch ignored his own urgent arousal, focusing on Mairi entirely.

And when he parted her thighs wide and lowered his head between them, his tongue and lips continuing their sensual onslaught, Mairi's ragged cry lanced through the chamber. She wreathed her fingers through his thick dark hair once again, tightening her grip on him as he pleasured her.

His flicking tongue drove her wild, and she sobbed his name as she arched, hard, against him.

Loch crawled over her then, propping himself up onto his elbows and cupping her face. He entered her slowly, inch by inch, in a sensual slide that made them both shudder and tremble. "Mairi," he breathed, staring deep into her eyes. "This is where I belong, lass ... buried deep inside ye."

“Aye,” she gasped. “I love ye, Loch … I’ve always loved ye.”

His eyes darkened at her declaration. “And I will ensure I’m worthy of yer love,” he vowed. Loch leaned in then, his lips slanting across hers, opening her mouth for a slow, intimate kiss that made her melt into the mattress. It was a kiss that touched the soul, one that exposed everything they both were. Their flaws and weaknesses—everything.

Moments later, Loch started moving inside her—and Mairi was lost.

29: WILL YE GIVE US YER BLESSING?

"CAN I FEED ye another honey cake, my love?"

"No ... another crumb and I'll burst." With a sigh of contentment, Mairi licked honey off her fingers and leaned back against the nest of pillows.

Sitting cross-legged upon the bed, and just as naked as she was, Loch grinned at her. "Well, ye won't mind if I take the last one then?"

"Go on."

Mairi watched him eat. Alison had cannily kept back a small basket of honey cakes, in case those who'd been on their feet all day—working in the inn—wanted a Yuletide treat once the last of the patrons departed.

After they'd recovered from their lovemaking, Loch had donned some clothes and gone down to the kitchen to retrieve the cakes.

The light from the nearby hearth bathed his strong, muscular body. Mairi noted that Loch was a little leaner than he'd been a few weeks ago. It still surprised her to know that he'd been pining.

For her.

Glancing her way, Loch met Mairi's eye and gave her a slow smile. "Like what ye see, lass?"

Mairi smiled back. "Aye," she murmured. "As well ye know ... ye conceited cockerel."

Loch threw back his head and laughed, and the rich depth of it made Mairi's smile widen. How she loved that sound.

Her gaze drifted down then, to where his rod was beginning to stiffen, and heat pooled between her thighs. Mairi's breathing grew shallow. She wanted him—again—and, from the looks of it, the desire was mutual.

Finishing the honey cake, Loch put the platter aside and stretched out next to her on the bed. Facing each other, they gazed into each other's eyes.

"It's late," Mairi murmured. "I suppose we should get some sleep."

"Neither of us will be resting tonight, my goddess," he murmured, his voice a low rumble that sent a thrill through her. "There will be plenty of time for that ... later."

Mairi wet her lips, aware that his attention was now focused on her mouth. Reaching out, she trailed a fingertip over the crisp dark hair on his chest. "No regrets then?" she whispered. She wasn't sure why she'd asked him that, only that flirtatious banter between them came easier than frankness, and a little of her old worries suddenly fluttered up.

Aye, he'd always been good at seduction and once hidden behind it.

She loved Loch fiercely, yet she was still learning to trust him again.

Loch caught her wandering hand and gently kissed the back of it. "None."

"And ye still wish to wed me?"

"As soon as it can be arranged." His gaze was level as it held hers. "I shall drag Father Hector from his bed at first light if need be."

"Welcome to yer new home," Loch announced as they trotted up the slope toward Duart Castle. Its high curtain walls loomed overhead, blocking out the pale sky. "Soon, ye will be the lady of this keep."

Mairi's heart kicked against her breastbone, nervousness fluttering in her belly. "Will the folk here accept me?"

The arm that Loch had wrapped around Mairi's midriff as they'd ridden from Craignure to Duart tightened. "Aye," he murmured. "Or they will deal with *me*." Hardness crept into his voice then, a reminder that the new Maclean clan-chief wasn't a man to be trifled with. "If anyone treats ye with disrespect, let me know."

They rode into the outer courtyard, where the snow had turned to dirty slush.

A large wolfhound came bounding out of the stables, barking excitedly.

"God's teeth," Mairi gasped. "What a beast."

Loch laughed. "Aye ... meet Luag. He was my father's hound ... and now has attached himself to me. I swear, the dog would climb into my bed if I let him."

A smile tugged at Mairi's lips. "Ye sound fond of the dog?"

"He's growing on me."

To their right, a tall, spare figure emerged from the chapel. Father Hector peered out at them, curious to see what had set the wolfhound to barking. Spying the laird, he gave a respectful nod. "Good morning, Maclean."

"Merry Yuletide, Father!" Loch called out. He then swung down from the saddle before helping Mairi down. "Ye have met Mairi Macquarie, have ye not?"

The chaplain nodded, his attention shifting to Loch's companion.

Mairi favored the man with a nervous smile. Father Hector had always intimidated her. Nonetheless, he'd shown great empathy for her father when he'd conducted his burial service, and she'd been grateful. "Morning, Father," she murmured. "Season's greetings."

"And to ye, lass," the chaplain replied. Father Hector's attention then swung back to Loch, his dark eyes bright with interest.

"Ready yerself for a wedding this morning, Father." Loch flashed him a wide smile. Father Hector's eyes snapped wide, yet ignoring his reaction, Loch continued.

"I'm about to give my bride-to-be a tour of her new home and inform my sister of the happy news … but we shall gather before the chapel shortly. Can ye—"

Loch broke off then, his gaze traveling across the courtyard, to where Jack had just emerged from the stables. He was with a tall, thin man with hawkish features, and appeared to be instructing him. Mairi recognized Jack's companion, for he'd wed one of her childhood friends.

"Jack! Struan!" Loch hailed the marshal and head groom. "Go and don yer finest clothes."

Jack arched his eyebrows. "And why is that?" he called back.

Loch put an arm around Mairi's shoulders, squeezing gently. "Because before the sun reaches noon, this fine woman will be my wife."

Jack strode toward them, a grin splitting his handsome face. "Why doesn't that come as a surprise?"

Reaching Loch, Jack clasped him in a hug. Drawing back, he favored Mairi with a warm smile. He winked at her then. "I never thought I'd see any woman bring my cousin to his knees."

Mairi smiled back, while Loch snorted. "Have ye seen Finn?"

Jack nodded. "I saw him go into the armory earlier."

"Go fetch him … I don't want ye two rogues to miss this."

"We won't," Jack assured him, still smiling. The cousin's gazes met and held then, and warmth suffused Mairi's chest at the affection that passed between them.

Jack and Finn were both incorrigible, yet she knew how attached Loch was to them. Mairi wanted those she loved to attend their wedding too—indeed, Alison and Tor would arrive soon, for they'd set off on foot from the inn.

Meanwhile, Father Hector was watching them all with a bewildered expression. Mairi didn't blame him—no doubt, today's wedding would be the talk of the castle, and Craignure, for weeks to come.

Struan stepped forward then and took Loch's horse by the reins. "I'll see to Falcon, Maclean," he said gruffly, even as his blue eyes twinkled.

Loch nodded to the head groom before turning to Mairi. "Are ye ready to be shown yer new home, mo chridhe?"

"Aye," Mairi murmured. She was doing her best to appear as if she was taking all of this in her stride. But, in truth, the butterflies in her stomach were still dancing, and despite that her nose, fingers, and toes were numb with cold this morning, she started to sweat.

Sensing Mairi's nervousness, Loch favored her with a soft smile and took her hand. "Come ... it'll be less intimidating than ye fear, ye'll see."

He led her across the slushy snow and up the steps into the keep, Luag following at his master's heel. They walked into an entrance hall first, which led into the large rectangular great hall.

Mairi's breathing caught as she stepped inside. She'd heard of this space yet had never set foot inside it until now. It was Saint Stephens, and the Yuletide decorations—garlands of ivy, wreaths of holly, and banks of candles—still decorated the hall. Two wolfhounds lazed in front of a great hearth, and servants glanced up from where they were setting places for the coming noon meal at the long trestle tables lining the hall.

"What do ye think?" Loch asked.

"It's grand," Mairi breathed, her gaze going to the table nearest the hearth, where a huge oaken chair with the Maclean crest carved into its back had pride of place. Her pulse then fluttered. "Too grand for me."

Loch harrumphed. "Nonsense."

They moved on from the hall, visiting the kitchens, the vast spence, the servants' lodgings, and the laundry. Loch then led her upstairs to his solar—a masculine space with sheepskins on the floor, weapons on the walls, and a massive stag head above the hearth. Afterward, he showed her the ladies' solar—a smaller chamber furnished with woven rugs, embroidered cushions, and pretty tapestries covering the cold stone walls.

“My mother decorated this solar,” Loch said, his voice softening. “These days, it’s only my sister who sometimes uses it … but when she does, she will welcome yer company, I’m sure.”

“Where is Lady Astrid?” Mairi asked.

A slight furrow appeared between Loch’s brows. “I don’t know … she might be resting in her bedchamber.” They left the ladies' solar, stepping out into the hallway illuminated by flickering cressets. “We shall find my sister shortly … but first, I’d like to show ye my mother’s pride … her Winter Garden.”

“A Winter Garden?” Mairi was intrigued.

With a smile, Loch took her by the hand once more and led the way down the hallway. The wolfhound padded along behind. The solid keep wrapped around an inner courtyard, and along the way, they passed arched windows that looked over a snow-carpeted square, where two bairns—servants’ children most likely—lobbed snowballs at each other. Their laughter and squeals echoed off stone.

Loch pushed a heavy door open then and guided Mairi up a set of slippery steps. They emerged into a small walled space.

Mairi’s breathing caught as she gazed upon it. Frosted with ice and a crisp layer of ermine snow, the Winter Garden was lovely indeed. Roses, bare of leaves and flowers this time of year, covered the walls, and neatly tended herbs lined the edge of the garden. At its center was a round vegetable plot, where kale and cabbage grew.

The garden wasn’t unattended this morning though—for a slender figure, wrapped in a heavy, fur-trimmed cloak, was helping herself to the largest of the cabbages.

Lady Astrid glanced up, her gaze traveling across the garden.

At the sight of Loch, she smiled, raising a gloved hand. “There ye are, brother,” she greeted him. “We were to visit the graveyard today, were we not?” Her attention shifted then to his companion, her gaze snapping wide. “Good morning, Mairi.”

"Greetings, Lady Astrid," Mairi replied, even as she tensed. Loch's sister was no doubt wondering why she was here.

"We shall visit the graveyard," Loch replied, smiling back. "But first, I'd like ye to attend my wedding."

Astrid's mouth opened, and she pushed herself to her feet. "What?"

Loch put an arm around Mairi's shoulders, drawing her close. "Ye probably never knew ... but a decade ago, when I went off to war, I left this lass behind" —his smile turned rueful— "I was a fool once ... but not any longer." He paused then, his gaze fusing with his sister's. "I love Mairi Macquarie and plan to spend the rest of my life with her. Will ye give us yer blessing, Astrid?"

Astrid stared back at him, a storm of emotion in her eyes.

Mairi's stomach clenched.

She couldn't help but worry that Loch overestimated his ability to break with convention and not pay the price. If Lady Astrid didn't accept her, life at Duart would be much harder than Loch anticipated.

But a heartbeat later, a warm smile lit up Astrid's face. "Of course."

30: HAPPY ENDINGS

THEY WERE THE only visitors to the graveyard today, for it lay under two feet of snow. However, most of the mossy tombstones still managed to peek through, glistening with icicles in the weak sunlight.

Mairi's breathing steamed as she crunched across the pristine crust of powder, heading toward a grave on the western edge of the small graveyard. To the east, the bulk of Duart Castle rose up against the sky, and beyond that, the Sound of Mull was the color of pewter. It hadn't snowed yet today, and the heavens had cleared, but the air was raw. The snow and ice wouldn't melt unless it warmed up.

Reaching her father's grave, Mairi crouched and brushed snow off the small stone cross. She then placed a holly wreath upon the hump of snow covering his grave. "I wish ye could have been here today, Da," she murmured. "What would ye have made of all of this?"

A wry smile tugged at her lips. No doubt, Athol Macquarie would have been bemused to see the arrogant Loch brought to his knees by Mairi. Like everyone else, Loch's proposal would have shocked him. However, he'd have rallied quickly, as Astrid had.

She knew he'd have given her his blessing. All her father had ever wanted was to see her happy. He'd no doubt marked how down she was after Loch went away, and sometimes she'd caught him watching her, his gaze sad. But he'd never said anything.

"I'd given up on ever having a happy ending, Da," she whispered, her throat thickening. Even now, she found it hard to accept she was really Loch Maclean's wife. Aye, they'd stood in the doorway to the chapel, surrounded by an awed crowd—Alison, Tor, Jack, Finn, and Lady Astrid among them—and had spoken their vows before Loch had hauled her into his arms for a passionate kiss. "Maybe I need to pinch myself."

Indeed, it hardly seemed real.

Just the day before, she'd been roasting geese for Yule and mulling wine for the patrons of *The Craignure Inn* while nursing a broken heart—and today, she was a laird's wife. Alison and Tor would run the inn from now on. She'd handed it over to them that morning. A new life yawned before her, one that both exhilarated and frightened her.

She wasn't sure she was ready for it—but she had Loch by her side. He'd look out for her and guide her through this foreign world, as would Lady Astrid. Loch's sister had found her a lovely surcote to wear for the ceremony. It had once belonged to Astrid and Loch's mother, and fortunately, the woman had been tall and statuesque like Mairi, not waiflike like her daughter.

The surcote, which Mairi still wore, was wine-red and threaded with silver. And she felt like a princess wearing it.

"Ye are always in my thoughts, Da," she said softly, rising to her feet and blinking away tears. "But I give myself solace by imagining that ye and Ma are together again ... I hope ye are both happy."

Turning, her gaze alighted on Loch and Astrid.

Brother and sister stood a few yards away watching her. They looked so different, one would never have thought they were related, except for their matching night-brown eyes. Him, swarthy and strong, and her, fragile and pale.

They'd waited respectfully while she laid a wreath on her father's grave before visiting their own kin.

Mairi smiled at them. She appreciated the gesture.

Wordlessly, the three of them walked into the heart of the graveyard, where the Maclean ruling family were buried—and there, side-by-side, were the tombstones of Iain and Gellise Maclean.

Loch and Astrid had also brought wreaths of holly and ivy for the dead. Mairi hung back a few yards as they approached the graves and laid the wreaths upon them. The bright red berries stood out against the whiteness of the snow, like spots of blood.

Loch knelt by the graves while his sister spoke a prayer for their parents. They were beautiful words, and Mairi's eyes prickled with fresh tears. Astrid's voice was thick with emotion; clearly, she'd adored her parents as much as Mairi had hers.

Cruelly, they'd all been taken too soon.

Lady Astrid rose to her feet then and gently squeezed her brother's shoulder before moving back from him, giving him some time alone with the dead. She crunched across the snow to where Mairi waited, favoring her with a watery smile. And then, to Mairi's surprise, she linked her arm through hers. "We are sisters now," she whispered.

Mairi smiled back and nodded, her throat tightening.

Meanwhile, Loch remained at the graves, his head bent. Time drew out, and the women waited. The cold bit through the layers of Mairi's clothing, and she could no longer feel her feet, yet she didn't complain.

Loch had told her about the letter he'd received from his father—and of the regret he carried regarding their relationship. This moment couldn't be rushed.

Eventually, Loch leaned forward, placed a hand on each gravestone, and murmured something. Getting to his feet, he brushed the snow off his knees, turned, and walked back to his wife and sister.

And as he approached, Mairi saw his cheeks were wet with tears.

"Loch," she breathed, her chest aching at his pain. "Are ye well?"

"Aye, lass," He favored her with a tender smile and stepped close, putting his arms around her. He leaned in then, his breath feathering across her ear as he added, "Better than I've ever been."

Loch took a sip of wine and glanced over at his wife.

Mairi sat next to him at the clan-chief's table, splendid in the dark-red surcote with silver trim. Under it, she wore a blue kirtle. Both garments were low-cut, revealing her magnificent cleavage.

Loch's pulse quickened. He looked forward to peeling both the surcote and kirtle off his wife later—but for the moment, he was content to sit here and feast his eyes on her.

Mairi *Maclean*.

It felt right to sit here, with her at his side.

The noise in the hall was deafening this evening. It was Saint Stephens and his wedding day, and so the cooks had done themselves proud—putting on a spread of mutton pie, blood sausage, braised venison, and an array of breads and cheeses.

Aye, the food was good, but Loch barely tasted it.

The only thing he could focus on was the beautiful woman seated to his right. She was his *anam cara*—his 'soul friend'. With her, he felt at peace, as if all was right in the world. They'd known each other for a long while, but for too many years, he'd taken her for granted.

He regretted that, would always regret it—but from this day on, he'd ensure Mairi always knew how much she meant to him.

"What do ye think of the wine?" he asked, meeting Mairi's eye.

"It's delicious … like everything on this table," she replied with a shy smile. "I've never seen such a spread."

"Enjoy it, my love," he said, his mouth quirking. "For it's in yer honor."

"I hope ye don't always eat like this … or I will soon be as fat as a Yuletide goose."

He laughed. "No, these rich dishes are reserved for special occasions."

Mairi's gaze held his, her golden-brown eyes full of curiosity. "Will I be expected to manage the cooks and servants now?"

He nodded, pleased by her question. He'd always appreciated Mairi's practical approach to things. "Aye ... they will answer to ye from now on ... and the skills ye employed at the inn will come in useful here. Ye are used to organizing a kitchen and stores and dealing with people." He paused then before reaching out and stroking her cheek. "Ye will find it easy, I think."

Mairi pulled a face. "Ye have much faith in me, Loch."

He smiled. "I do ... and it is merited." He withdrew his hand then and picked up his goblet of bramble wine. "However, ye needn't fear ... Astrid and I will assist ye until ye find yer feet here."

Her mouth curved. "Thank ye."

Loch leaned back in his carven chair, watching as his wife helped herself to a mutton pie. She took a large bite before licking the gravy off her fingers. The gesture was unconsciously sensual, and Loch's belly tightened. Mairi stoked a fire in him that would never be quenched. He'd never be able to get enough of her.

Taking another sip of wine, Loch enjoyed the moment before realizing that something was missing.

The disquiet that had plagued him his entire life was absent.

In the past, whenever he retreated into his own thoughts, agitation surfaced. It was a sensation he'd always sought to escape, first through rebellion, then by throwing himself into the Bruce's cause. But it didn't matter what he did, the unease had never lessened. Upon his return to Mull, he'd hoped weaving peace between the Macleans and the Mackinnons might chase the uneasiness away—yet it hadn't.

Only making things right, first with his sister, and then with the woman he loved, had slayed his demons.

Loch's gaze traveled then, down the clan-chief's table to where Astrid sat opposite Jack and Finn. His sister ate with small, delicate mouthfuls, yet he was relieved to see that she *was* eating, for she was still far too thin.

Astrid's gaze was upon Jack as he argued with Finn about something, her dark eyes sharp with observation. His sister had managed this castle well after their father died. Mairi would now be chatelaine of Duart, yet he knew Astrid would grow bored and restless confined to the ladies' solar to while away her days at weaving and embroidery. His sister was good at strategy and understood what motivated people, both skills he would use to help him rule.

He caught a snatch of Jack and Finn's conversation then. Jack had fastened on the Mackinnons and, like a terrier with a rat in its jaws, wouldn't let go.

"'The Butcher of Dun Ara' will want vengeance for the breaking of a promise, mark my words," he muttered, stabbing a piece of venison with his eating knife. "We'd be fools to sit around and wait for it."

"What would ye have us do then?" Astrid asked, clearly unable to hold her tongue any longer. "Raid Mackinnon lands ... slaughter their women and bairns?"

Jack's features tightened, while next to him, Finn's lips thinned. He gave Astrid a cold look then, and she responded with a lip curl.

"Ye could have been wedded to that shit-bag," Jack growled. "Ye should *want* us to strike him before he takes out his revenge."

"And throw our clans into open warfare? I think not," Astrid replied. "We'd be wiser to ensure the northern edges of our lands are well defended ... so that more of our livestock doesn't go missing ... so that we *show* him we are watching."

"Meanwhile, Dounarwyse is at risk," Jack muttered. A flush had appeared across his high cheekbones, a sign his temper was rising. "When Kendric Mackinnon comes for us... it'll be my brother's castle he'll strike."

"Rae knows he defends our border," Loch spoke up. "He has asked me for more warriors to guard the land around Faing Burn ... and he shall receive them."

"That's not enough," Jack ground out, his fingers gripping the edge of the table. "We need to storm Dun Ara ... and cut the butcher's throat."

"That won't happen, Jack," Loch said, his voice chilling now. "And I'm rapidly tiring of yer bloodthirsty talk."

Jack's auburn brows knitted together at this rebuke, a muscle feathering in his jaw, yet he held his tongue. He'd been in good spirits after the wedding ceremony—but the discussion now had soured his mood.

"All the same, Loch ... doesn't Kendric Mackinnon's silence make ye nervous?" Finn asked then, picking up his goblet and swirling his wine.

"A little," Loch admitted. "He'll be vexed ... and he *will* want to make me pay for breaking our agreement." He glanced over at Astrid. His sister was frowning. "But I don't regret going back on my word," he added, watching as Astrid's brow smoothed. "Some things are too precious to sacrifice."

A hand squeezed his knee then, and Loch shifted his attention to his wife, to find her favoring him with a soft smile.

Her eyes were luminous and full of love.

EPILOGUE: CALLING TO YE

Three months later ...

WITH THE WIND in her hair and a clear blue sky arching overhead, Mairi couldn't help but grin.

Standing at Loch's side upon the high sculpted ridge of Dùn da Ghaoithe, she felt like a kestrel, soaring above the world. This mountain, the second highest on the isle, towered over the eastern side of Mull. The peak, 'the fort of two winds', was visible from both Craignure and Duart Castle, and during the winter, its long ridge glittered white.

This was the first time Mairi had seen it at such close quarters. When Loch discovered that she'd never visited the mountain, he'd promised to take her there.

And now that spring had arrived, he had.

It had been quite a climb to reach this point, and they'd had to dismount Loch's stallion and walk up the scree-covered slope to the top, but it was worth it.

A few yards away, Luag lay, panting.

"Look," she gasped, pointing east. "There's Duart Castle ... although it looks tiny from up here." Indeed, the fortress was a speck on the shore with the glittering water of the Sound of Mull behind it.

Loch huffed a laugh. "Aye ... like a bairn's toy."

He put an arm around Mairi's shoulders, drawing her close. The feel of his strong body against hers, and his smell—crisp and clean with the darker undertones of smoke and leather—made her senses sharpen.

A companionable silence fell between husband and wife as they continued to look out over the folds of hills that rolled down to the eastern coast.

However, eventually, Loch spoke. "I finally received a missive from the Mackinnon yestereve."

Mairi glanced up, surprised. "Ye didn't say?" After Loch had written to Kendric Mackinnon, informing him that he wouldn't be wedding Astrid, after all, the clan-chief had remained ominously silent.

He sighed. "Aye ... well, I didn't want Astrid to overhear."

Mairi frowned. "It wasn't a friendly missive then?"

"No ... he demands I uphold my promise, or he shall take back the lands north of Dounarwyse. His daughter is set to wed the son of Aonghas MacDonald of Sleat within the week ... and he will ask his new ally to join him against us. He also threatened to sack Dounarwyse Castle itself ... and to take it as his own."

Mairi tensed. She'd expected Mackinnon to threaten to raze the land around Faing Burn, but to openly admit to gathering allies and threatening an attack on Dounawyse was bold indeed. "Do ye believe he'll do as he says?"

Loch's expression grew grim. "He earned his name for a reason, Mairi ... I'd be a fool to underestimate him."

"So, what will ye do?" Her pulse quickened then. "Ye won't hand Astrid over to him, will ye?"

Loch's jaw tightened. "Never."

Relief swamped her, although she shouldn't have worried he'd change his mind again about that. Over the past months, brother and sister had grown close. Mairi often found them seated together in the evenings in the clan-chief's solar, feet up on settles, bantering and talking about daily business.

Loch and Astrid might not have looked alike, yet they shared the same dry sense of humor, the same sense of irony—which could easily slide into cynicism if left unchecked. They were good for each other, and it warmed Mairi to see them bond.

"What will ye do then?"

"More of what I've already been doing," he replied.

It pleased Mairi that there was no irritation in his voice when he responded to her questions. These days, Loch didn't chafe at hearing his womenfolk voice opinions. He and Mairi often discussed clan politics. Aye, he hadn't mentioned the Mackinnon's missive to her, but that was to spare upsetting Astrid. His sister had a tough shell—and was highly capable—yet her reaction to the betrothal her brother had made for her revealed that she was deeply sensitive.

"I've sent Jack north to warn his brother about the Mackinnon's threats," he went on. "I've already provided Rae with more warriors ... but I can spare another twenty if he requires them."

Mairi nodded, meeting Loch's eye once more. "So, Jack took Mackinnon's missive badly?"

"Aye." Loch grimaced. "I was treated to a rant about how we need to gather our allies ... how we must rally the MacLeods to our side and lay siege to Dun Ara. It was a relief to send him on his way."

Mairi's heart kicked against her ribs. "Ye won't attack the Mackinnons, will ye?"

"I'd prefer not to ... not without good cause," Loch replied. He lifted a hand, brushing her hair off her cheek. There was a stiff breeze up here, although wrapped up in woolen cloaks and still sweating from the climb, Mairi barely noticed. "I'm not against fighting when I must ... but these days, peace holds more appeal. I didn't come home to spill my clansmen's blood."

Mairi nodded, relieved that he planned to proceed with caution. However, something in his tone intrigued her, and the way he was looking at her now made her pulse quicken. Loch wore a soft look upon his face, one she knew well.

"Aye?" she murmured. "And why did ye come home then, Loch Maclean ... was this misty isle calling to ye?"

His lips lifted at the corners. "No, lass ... *ye* were. I was just too blind to see it."

And with that, he lowered his head, cupped her face with his hands, and kissed her deeply.

The End

HISTORICAL NOTES

Most of this novel takes place at Duart Castle on the Isle of Mull. This magnificent fortress still stands today. Dating back to the 13th century, it's the seat of clan Maclean. The castle's position was a strategic one, for it sits upon a high crag at the end of a peninsula jutting into the Sound of Mull, where it guards the channel between Mull and the mainland.

The 14th-century keep was built by Chief Lachlan Lubanach Maclean. On the vulnerable landward side, the walls are 29 feet (9m) high and 10 feet (3m) thick, while the walls facing the sea are thinner, ranging from 5 to 9 feet (1.8m to 2.4m).

The castle fell into ruin from the 18th century, until it was completely refurbished in 1911 by Sir Fitzroy Maclean.

I have played around with history a bit with this novel. I wanted to call my hero Lachlan to fit in with the real clan-chief (there were quite a few Lachlans in the Maclean family tree, which gets confusing), but I already have written a Lachlan before in THE OUTLAW'S BRIDE. So, I called our hero Loch instead (and in my opinion, the name really suits him!). Lachlan Maclean's wife was called Mary (hence my choice to name our heroine Mairi), however, their story was a little different from mine.

Lachlan had to obtain a papal dispensation to marry Mary Macdonald. It was said theirs was a love match, and her father was persuaded to allow it only after Lachlan kidnapped him!

I also chose to set this story a few decades earlier than when Lachlan Maclean would have ruled, to tie the novel in with the Battle of Bannockburn. Although the first mention of a Maclean at Duart Castle was in 1367, historical records are sketchy, to say the least. As such, it's likely that he wasn't the first Maclean clan-chief to live at Duart Castle.

ADDITIONAL NOTES

I always listen to music when I write—it helps me access emotion and transports me into my story world. For THE LASS HE LEFT BEHIND, there were two tracks that I listened to on repeat.

Here they are:

We will go home (Song of Exile) from the King Arthur soundtrack:
https://www.youtube.com/watch?v=fzjjNpzFa2Y

Ailein Duinn
https://www.youtube.com/watch?v=HJMC2keqX_o&t=24s

I use the words from 'Ailein duinn' in Chapter Nine of the novel. It's a tragic traditional Scottish Gaelic lament that was perfect for Mairi to sing alone.

The story goes that 'Ailein duinn' (Dark-haired Alan) was written for Ailean Moireasdan (Alan Morrison) by his fiancée, Annag Chaimbeul (Annie Campbell). Ailean was a sea captain from the Isle of Lewis. One spring, he left Stornoway to go to Scalpay, Harris, where he was to be engaged to Annag. Unfortunately, they sailed into a storm and all the crew sank with the vessel, off the coast of the Shiant Islands.

Broken-hearted, Annag composed this lament for her lost love. However, she lost her will to live and died a few months afterward. There wasn't enough soil on the barren island of Scalpay to bury her there, so her father took Annag's coffin by boat to a cemetery on the main island of Harris. But a storm blew her coffin off her father's boat, and it washed up on the same island, where Ailein's body was found. (Source: https://en.wikipedia.org/wiki/Ailein_duinn)

In this novel, Mairi and Loch dress up at The Morrígan and The Dagda for Samhain. The coupling of these two ancient Celtic warrior gods was indeed an important part of the Samhain festival, which the Celts celebrated to mark the beginning of a new year.

I also mention the Headless Horseman of Mull in this story. There are many tales from around the world of such a ghost, yet the most prominent Scottish one comes from the Isle of Mull. It concerns a man named Ewen of the Little Head (Eoghann a'Chinn Bhig), decapitated in a clan battle at Glen Cainnir on the Isle of Mull. The battle denied him any chance to be a chieftain.

But Ewen's ghost is unable to rest in peace, and ever since that day, the specter of a headless rider on a black horse is reported to ride through Glen More between dusk and dawn. In particular, it is believed that his appearance to one of the Maclean clan, or the sound of his horses' hooves galloping around the clan seat at Moy by Lochbuie, is an omen that a member of that family is about to die.
https://en.wikipedia.org/wiki/Headless_Horseman
https://thehazeltree.co.uk/2015/05/16/glen-more-and-the-headless-horseman/

As always, I hope these notes give you an insight into the research I do, and into the rich culture and history my novels anchor themselves on.

DIVE INTO MY BACKLIST!

Check out my printable reading order list on my website: https://www.jaynecastel.com/printable-reading-list

ABOUT THE AUTHOR

Multi-award-winning author Jayne Castel writes epic Historical and Fantasy Romance. Her vibrant characters, richly researched historical settings, and action-packed adventure romance transport readers to forgotten times and imaginary worlds.

Jayne is the author of a number of best-selling series. A hopeless romantic in love with all things Scottish, she writes romances set in both Dark Ages and Medieval Scotland.

When she's not writing, Jayne is reading (and re-reading) her favorite authors, cooking Italian feasts, and going on long walks with her husband. She's from New Zealand, but now lives in Edinburgh, Scotland.

Connect with Jayne online:
www.jaynecastel.com
www.facebook.com/JayneCastelRomance
https://www.instagram.com/jaynecastelauthor/
Email: contact@jaynecastel.com

Milton Keynes UK
Ingram Content Group UK Ltd.
UKHW040959040324
438885UK00005B/326